# THE WILD ONES

## ABEL'S APOCALYPSE BOOK TWO

Bryan Dean

This is a work of fiction. Names, characters, businesses, places, events, locales, and incidents are either the products of the author's imagination or used in a fictitious manner. Any resemblance to actual persons, living or dead, or actual events is purely coincidental. All rights reserved. No part of this publication may be reproduced, distributed, or transmitted in any form or by any means, including photocopying, recording, or other electronic or mechanical methods, without the prior written permission of the publisher, except in the case of brief quotations embodied in critical reviews and certain other non-commercial uses permitted by copyright law.

All rights reserved. Except as permitted under the U.S. Copyright Act of 1976, no part of this book may be reproduced, scanned, transmitted, or distributed in any form or by any means, or stored in a database or retrieval system, without the prior written permission of the publisher. Please do not participate in or encourage piracy of copyrighted materials in violation of the author's rights.

© 2023 Bryan Dean.

ISBN: 978-1-7352793-8-1

Contact the author via email: CLELUTZ11@gmail.com

# ACKNOWLEDGEMENTS

I'd like to thank my friends, family, and you for your support. A special thanks to Darline, Sharon, Steve, Russ, Tim, Charley, and Sean. Without your encouragement, this simply doesn't happen.

To the American Military: Without you standing watch over this great nation, this book may not have been possible. You do what few among us have the courage to do. Thank you.

Edited by
Booked for Good Edits
Booked4good@gmail.com
Thank you for your hard work and guidance.

Cover designed by: Kelly A. Martin
www.kam.design

Kelly, you are a master at your craft!

Image Credits:
DepositPhotos/alessandroguerr, Depositphotos/monkeybusiness, DepositPhotos/everlite1knight, Neostock, Shuuterstock/Vilmos Varga

## Chapter 1

One Week Prior To The Fall Of New York

Family Handler Li Chok's gaze remained unbroken. He'd been in possession of the package for over half an hour, but remained skeptical of discovering its contents. The innocuous brown box held something of substantial weight, but had cleared the explosives, biological threat, and corrosive substance tests administered in the lower levels of the Ministry of Civil Affairs building. But the sender's address confused and worried him.

Addressed to him as classified, it originated from the Chinese Consulate in New York City and was mailed the exact day they'd lost contact with those same offices. It arrived, according to security, with the Consulate's standard weekly intelligence. The hard-copy transfer, sent via Chinese Government Currier, ensured America's counterintelligence apparatus wouldn't intercept the documents. It was slower than electronic intelligence transfers, but far more secure.

Li had never received a communiqué directly from the Consulate, let alone the Consul General's Office. He'd never interacted with the Consulate at any level, instead receiving orders exclusively from Da Cik, the Minister of Civil Affairs. He was a handler of families, nothing more. Outside of interfacing with his assigned list of delegates dispatched overseas, determining the disposition of rogue delegate's families, and ensuring their *safety*, he held no decision-making authority in matters under his purview. Yet, the package sat on his desk.

The calming exercises he'd been employing hadn't reigned in his anxiety. After hearing the strange reports of civil unrest occurring in America, coupled with treasonous whispers of mid-level bureaucrats that a Chinese scientist may be at the root of that unrest, Li had quietly distanced himself from his last assignment. The execution of Su's family had been a subdued event, carried out in the Family Center's basement at midnight. It lacked the usual fanfare associated with what the CCP considered a noble action of guarding national security. But he'd just been thrust into China's burning political spotlight. Once security notified his superiors of the package, an investigation into why he received it would ensue. He understood the Party's ranking members would soon regard him with suspicion. This package had shortened his lifespan by decades.

Cognizant he was under the watchful eye of the security team, which monitored his every move via the camera mounted in the ceiling of his unremarkable office, Li lifted his arm from his lap. Its heaviness, combined with its unwillingness to move towards the box, forced Li to sit forward and marshal his declining nerve. Not opening the box would prove equally as detrimental as its abrupt, unexplained appearance.

A sudden spike of anger urged his hand forward. The snap of his box cutter's blade piercing the thick packing tape forced his free hand to his brow to interrupt the path of the sweat marching down his wrinkled forehead. With a violent slash, his blade freed the box's flaps. Li flinched, expecting an equally aggressive reaction from within the mysterious container.

But nothing happened; it had opened in the same mundane, uneventful manner as the thousands of other boxes he'd opened at this very desk. Yet, this package seemed anything but mundane.

"It is only a box, you fool. Stop acting like a frightened child," he chided before plunging his hand into the package.

Li's face pinched, his mind unable to make sense of the object in his hand, his head tilted as if a fresh point of view would bring clarity. It didn't. The heavy glass cylinder, standing no more than four inches from its base, a measurement, he assumed, matched by its circumference, held a medicinal vial within a perfectly sized void. At its top and bottom were silver discs with small metallic spikes embedded in the thick glass, which appeared to prevent the vial from traveling vertically while the cylinder's tight confines stifled left-to-right movement. Its construction so meticulous, he'd hardly noticed the seam where its lid was secured to its body.

Li set the cylinder on his desk, causing the amber liquid within the vial to quiver, and carefully tipped the empty box to its side and snorted derisively. A plain white envelope had been taped to its bottom. "Of course, Consul General Bie would send an explanation."

He made a show of removing the envelope, sure to allow the camera to capture his slightest of movements. With the letter laid flat on his desk, granting the camera an unobstructed view, he read a message which pulled the air from his lungs.

*Respectable Handler Li, I'm writing to you on behalf of Doctor Su, and have enclosed his final, and corrected, work for you to deliver, personally, to President Zi. Su insisted his work be delivered by you to atone for his earlier failure and the disgrace he brought upon our great country. His sincerest hope is this small gesture also eases the burden his failure placed on your gracious and honorable shoulders.*

*Access to the vial is gained by placing the cylinder on a sturdy flat surface, pressing down firmly, and turning the top one quarter left.*

*Respectfully Yours,*

*Consul General Bie*

Li's office door burst open the same instant he finished the letter. He wasn't surprised. The letter's mention of President Zi mandated a swift and harsh reaction by the security forces monitoring his office. He'd done well to allow them to read the letter. Had he not, but then requested an audience with Zi, they would have summarily executed him.

"Open it!" A guard with stony features yelled as more guards filtered into his office while others took up positions on his sides, effectively surrounding him.

Li knew what was happening. He'd become the equivalent of the food testers of ancient times, ensuring the emperor's meal was free of poison. He nodded, forcing a broad smile and fixing it in place.

Any action at this point, even a bead of sweat, would cost him his life if the guards determined it to be a sign of trepidation.

"May I?" he asked while dipping his head toward the letter. "The instructions for opening the cylinder — I require them."

The first guard to enter his office narrowed his eyes, then nodded his approval.

Li slid the letter next to the cylinder and followed the directions by placing his right hand on top of the smooth glass surface while gripping it tight in his left.

The muffled *tink* of fracturing glass preceded Li's startled yelp by a millisecond. He yanked his hand from the cylinder and shook it, trying to relieve the lingering burn.

"What have you done!" a guard yelled as the others inched closer.

But Li didn't answer. The small metal spike protruding from the fractured glass had seized his attention. The guard yelled again, but his voice was muffled, unintelligible as Li bent to inspect the object closer. Was it? Yes, it was a small hollow shaft that had impaled his hand, and it was smeared with his blood. But the amber liquid bubbling from the shaft is what held his gaze. Was the vial now half empty?

Sergeant Bue, the guard in command, recoiled at the sound of Li's teeth grinding, then startled as the waif of a man slowly raised his head, pinning his stare to Bue.

"Sergeant," Li began, "you haven't brought enough guards."

Bue's features hardened. Was this insignificant bureaucrat threatening him? Bue surged forward, shot his arm over Li's desk, and grabbed the man by his shirt's collar. His jaw hinged open the same instant Li's fist crashed through his forearm, separating it at the elbow.

The security forces froze as their sergeant's incredulous stare lingered on his ruined arm. The swift and volatile stroke had removed the appendage with surgical precision, creating a perfectly smooth wound, which took seconds to bleed.

Li capitalized on their hesitation and lunged at the guard to his right. The unsuspecting man startled when he suddenly found himself staring into black, menacing eyes, then crumbled to the floor, his heart still beating in Li's hand.

Li watched the violence unfold through an ever-collapsing tunnel. The spray of blood, jolt of his fist impacting flesh, and screams of dying men seemed to be viewed from a spectator's seat, high above the battlefield. Yet, he could plainly see his hands inflicting the devastation.

His rational mind disconnected as the urge to bite his victims overwhelmed the sliver of humanity it was tethered to. Li's rapid evolution culminated with an instinctual thrust of his gaping maw towards his first victim's neck. It had to be the neck — it was the shortest route to the brain.

***

From his predatory crouch, Li glared at the Great Hall of The People. His view from the sweeping, ornate roof of the Ministry of

Civil Affairs building was unobstructed by the city's crowded skyline. He yearned to rampage through Beijing's streets, tear the Great Hall apart brick by brick, and claim his rightful place atop the rubble of yesterday's government.

With a clack of his teeth, he forced himself to remain patient. He couldn't defeat the Hall's countless guards, at least not alone. But his soldiers, the ones being created in the bowels of the building beneath his feet, would be all he needed to overcome the forces standing watch over the Great Hall.

This reality made him smile.

# Chapter 2

"Who authorized it?" General Malloy yelled as his fist slammed against the conference table, silencing his command team's bickering.

None of them spoke.

"Am I to believe that two dozen of our finest aircraft were fueled, armed, flown to New York City, where they released their ordnance, destroyed the city, returned to base, and not one person in this room knows who authorized the mission? A mission which squandered our diminishing resources while risking the lives of pilots whose value in this war is immeasurable?"

"General," Colonel Rey began, breaking the awkward silence, "maybe we shelve discussing the bombing and focus instead on lifting the new ROEs. They've made it nearly impossible to maintain operational readiness. We should revisit our willingness to abandon warfighters for simply being exposed to a hot-zone for an extended length of time. We possess the ability to check them for signs of infection. CENTCOM has contacted hundreds of *displaced* soldiers — not one of our points of contact has contracted the infection by simply being trapped in a hot-zone."

Malloy gave a slight nod. Rey had answered his question. "So, it was you."

Rey's head slumped. Then, with chin to chest, he answered, "Yes."

"Colonel, please explain your reasoning. Did the good Lord Himself whisper in your ear that by bombing New York City, the infection would magically disappear? Because any other reason is unacceptable."

"I lost soldiers!" Rey snapped, his chin jutting in defiance. "That cluster of a strategy cost us dozens of the finest soldiers this country has ever seen. I refused to let CENTCOM sacrifice another life."

The room bristled at Rey's admission while Malloy restrained his urge to shoot the insubordinate jackass. They were already struggling to maintain combat readiness; killing Rey would only weaken them further.

"Colonel, we *all* lost soldiers during that operation. And your actions ensured thousands more will die. I can think of one in particular. He was perfectly positioned to lead our Special Operation Force directly to both of our patient zeros. His name was Blum, Sergeant Blum, and he'd commandeered a hardened site at the edge of Central Park. I was going to tap him to lead the SOF. Instead, *I* had to tell him his country had forsaken him. Now, after your little temper tantrum, I haven't been able to reach him. Tell me, what does that mean?"

Rey searched Malloy's eyes for deception. He found bitter truth. "I, I was unaware we had assets on the ground..."

"Colonel, stop speaking. Now, since you view yourself as the all-knowing rod of justice, you're in command of building our SOF.

Their objective is to secure both targets. DARPA cares very little that *you* destroyed the city and exponentially increased the risk. They want these men secured A-SAP."

Malloy tapped his laptop's *enter* key and spun to face the room's monitor as Su and Sampson's faces flashed.

"We believe Sampson Jennings to be patient zero for the Omega variant. This is one of several dozen booking photos. He now looks like this," he said as he advanced to the next picture, a grainy screen-grab from one of the countless surveillance videos he'd featured in. "As you can see, the infection has changed him, but only to a degree. This is Doctor Su Zain," he continued as he advanced through the slideshow, "and we believe him to be our true patient zero — Alpha variant. We *must* find this man. You'll forgive the lack of our usual Target Package. Their histories are irrelevant. The slivers of useful INTEL we possess include they're preference for hunting at night. DARPA is working to understand why and develop a strategy to capitalize on this behavior. To be clear, they *will* venture into daylight, especially Omega variants, but both become dramatically more active in the evening. Also, each successive generation exhibits a marked decline in cognitive ability as well as motor skills. Clear as mud, I know. But the INTEL should guide our strategy. Distribute their photographs to every single set of boots left standing. I'll stress, our understanding of the infected is constantly evolving. This evolution will require real-time adjustments to strategy. Remain flexible, communicate clearly, and we save lives."

Malloy sat quietly as the screen faded to black, then locked Rey in a withering glare. "As for rescinding our ROEs. We have! You were a few days early pulling that trigger. We'll begin reaching out to our affected personnel immediately. However, many of them have established militias, joined communities, or otherwise secured their safety. They've been more effective at combating the infected than the entire U.S. military and we will *not* force them to abandon their strategies. We will, instead, partner with them to relieve the pressure building on our forces. We will arm them, feed them, and set them loose on this scourge. These men and women are proven survivors... true warriors. They will receive our full support."

The General paused, but held Rey in his contemptuous glare before moving the briefing forward. "Colonel Stevens, what's our infrastructure status?"

Stevens cleared his throat, more to break the tension than prepare his throat to speak. "We've secured most of the power grid, but we're going to struggle to continue producing power to feed it. Our efforts to secure the operators and their families in onsite compounds were successful, but raw materials are dwindling. We're developing a solution but have no timeline. The Northeast is dark. Parts of PA and WV are also without power. Water is still pumping, but, out of an abundance of caution, we've issued a boil alert. Obviously, if power goes, so too, does the water. The internet went down yesterday and is a low priority. Cell service is non-existent. We're helping where we can, but by the nature of the cell network, it's an overwhelming task. I hold little optimism in our infrastructure's ability, at any level, to withstand a storm, or storms, of any meaningful intensity."

"We'll lean on our local assets once we supply and organize them. Provide a list of priorities by geography to Colonel Spiegel. His team is spearheading our efforts with our displaced personnel." Malloy would usually solicit feedback or field questions at this point in a briefing, but he was still at war with his urge to execute Rey. They'd covered the urgent topics. He'd heard enough.

"We failed our country when we chose not to neutralize these monsters when we became aware of them. We will not fail her again. Dismissed."

## Chapter 3

Alan Williams' head snapped up, the stench too strong for his dozing mind to ignore, jolting him from his ill-advised slumber. Only one thing emitted this disgusting odor and its intensity sent Alan scrambling along the wall for the alarm bell a mere twenty feet away.

His guard post, positioned on the community's northeastern-most point, the one the community's leaders determined would be least likely to experience an attempted breach, was basically a fire watch outpost. Surrounded by heavily treed land, it sat at the bend of Minsi Trail Road and over a mile and a half from the Turnpike barricade.

Alan was sure its remote, seemingly unimportant location was the reason he'd been stationed there. But the increasing stench told a different story. They'd underestimated the monsters.

The struggle to stand and then accelerate his obese frame to full stride had taken too long and far too much effort for a man of thirty-four. His battle to catch a breath turned urgent when pain shot down his left arm — the tightness in his chest, he realized, wasn't from exertion. It was the widow maker his doctor had promised.

His legs weakened as he neared the bell. He only had to strike it once with the hammer tethered to his belt. But his girth buckled his knees as he grasped and raised the tool over his head. With the last of his will, and images of his wife and newborn son burnt into his mind, Alan keeled over — dead before his clammy body slammed to the elevated wooden walkway.

***

Sampson sniffed the air. The scent he'd been following turned from tantalizing to stale as a heavy thud rattled the barrier he and his growing army were pressed against. Although not as sweet, the meet would still be warm and would sate his soldiers' growing hunger.

With a deep inhale, Sampson's head tilted. A feral grin chipped the blood caked on his cheeks, sending it fluttering to his chest in flakes of every size. He'd found more food cowering behind the fortification.

Sampson pushed on the wall and projected to the few soldiers whose minds he could still reach to join him. He knew the others would follow.

***

Jerry stopped to light one of his last Marlboros and cursed under his breath. Tomorrow he'd be smoking his stash of generic cigarettes. "Like smoking pencil shavings!"

If he'd known last week's supply run to the convenient store in Haven would be the last the community leaders were planning for at least another month, he would have rationed his Marlboros more diligently. But smoking, drinking, and guard duty were the only things to do since they'd lost power. "Somebody better get this shit under control because no one wants to see me without nicotine in my system!" he groused, as he restarted his trek to check on Alan.

"Jesus, ya fat bastard, what the hell are you cooking up there?" he yelled, as Alan's perch came into view the same instant the stench of earth tinged with chemicals and rot reached him.

Jerry's stride faltered. Alan was always quick with an equally biting retort when his balls were being busted. "What's wrong, did I hurt your bacon-saturated feelings?" Still nothing.

His pace lengthened to long strides. His friend would never miss an opportunity to verbally spar with his longtime neighbor. They'd done it nearly every day over the fifteen years they'd lived next to one another.

After a frantic search for his flashlight, Jerry lit the spot where Alan should have been. "Where the hell are you?" he hissed. "If you're sleeping again, I'll kick your flabby ass."

But Jerry knew. His gut told him Alan was in trouble. The realization pushed him to a sprint. Steps from the catwalk's ladder, his flashlight's beam swept over an enormous form crumpled at the base of the alarm bell. "Holy shit! Al, are you alright? Talk to me!" he shouted, as he reached the ladder's second rung.

With his head tilted and eyes pinned on his friend's body, the shards of plywood exploding from the wall followed an unmolested path to his craned neck. On impulse, his hands raced to the wound and sent his body tumbling from the ladder. Sampson's soldiers swarmed his flailing carcass the instant it bounced on the hard pack.

\*\*\*

Sampson marched his soldiers through the remnants of their conquest. There was ample food here, but not enough to settle this land. The search for hunting grounds would continue, now with many new recruits.

# Chapter 4

*I'm still not talking to you,* Abe's scrawled note read.

"It's been a week, Abe. This is ridiculous... *you're being ridiculous!*"

Lu watched as Abe scribbled furiously. She already knew what he was writing. *You let her eat the last of my bacon and she scratched my gun! My very expensive CZ Scorpion, which I didn't tell her she could use. I'm never talking to either of you again!*

"The apocalypse didn't cure your high cholesterol, so I let her have the bacon. She apologized for the scratch. Plus, she used it to save my life!"

Lu waited quietly as Abe scratched his pencil through the pages of his small notebook. If she attempted to rush the pace of their argument Abe would merely write slower. *It was my bacon! And don't be so dramatic. She was probably shooting at the sky while running away. I've shot that gun a dozen times, never a scratch... not ONE!*

"Whatever! I'm getting dinner ready. What do you want?"

*Freeze-dried lasagna. An MRE for Nic. I'll get the food. Keep an eye on your friend!*

\*\*\*

"Please, Lu. Not another MRE. They have so much sodium in them I'm swelling like a deer tick. And they taste awful!"

Nic spun at the sound of fingers snapping, and found Abe holding a note, inches from her face. *I picked this especially for you. Menu 17, pork sausage patty, maple flavored. Not moxorella but still YUMMY!*

"You're an ass!" Nic yelled while swatting at the note. "Lu, can't you make some extra lasagna? Please, I'm *begging* you!"

"He locked the storage room and hid the key. Nic, honey, it's better than not eating. Try to make the best of it. He'll calm down. Just give him a few more days."

"Wait! Isn't lasagna high in cholesterol?"

Nic glared at Abe with a spiteful grin as he scribbled. *Ha! Nice try, meatless!*

A hard knock on the door cut off Nic's retort as Abe was quick to retreat from the kitchen and rush to answer.

*Are you here to try to get me to talk to Lu and Nic?*

Finn read Abe's note with a mixture of confusion and amusement. "No, I'm not. But you're an actual piece of work, Abe. I'm here because Stanley's exile starts in about thirty minutes. Figured you'd want to help see him off."

"Hell yeah, I want to see that. You can tell Nic and Lu; I'm sure they'll want to watch, too."

"Um," Finn began while glancing over Abe's shoulder, "they're about ten feet away."

"Then you won't have to walk far to tell them. I'll meet you at the main gate!"

\*\*\*

## The Wild Ones

The stream of people heading for the gate surprised Abe. A week had passed, yet the grim set of their features spoke to their determination to see this through, to cast out one of their own. They'd taken no pleasure in the verdict, which amounted to a death sentence if Forward Operating Base Olmsted denied Stanley's request for safe harbor. Nor would they shed a tear at his leaving. The man bore the responsibility for the deaths of two of their friends and had nearly destroyed the community. This was as close to an eye for an eye justice as they could stomach.

The soft rumble of idling engines grew louder as Abe rounded the corner from his street onto the road leading to the main gate and the scene broke his stride. A caravan, at least five vehicles strong, was waiting to exit.

A glance through the gathered crowd, searching for someone he cared to talk to, ended when he found Randy a few yards away.

"What's happening?"

"Stan caused a mutiny, fifteen people in all. Bina talked to Crystal. She said he's been telling everyone that'll listen that moving to the military base is their safest option. And that you'll get us all killed because you're a Neanderthal."

"Who's Crystal?"

"Stan's wife. You really don't talk to anyone, do you?"

"Ha," Finn began, startling Abe as he walked up behind him, "the base is going to refuse his request for access. I talked to the base CO last night. He told me if Stanley shows up, they're going to redirect him to the FEMA refugee camp set up in Great Northern Mall. Awful place from what I've been hearing."

"Oh man, he'll have plenty of people to *connect* with." Abe glanced at Finn. "So, speaking of camps, when are your families moving in?"

"They were cleared to depart yesterday. I got the message last night. We're escorting Stan to FOB Olmsted. He thinks he's special. He doesn't know we're doing it for our families. And he has no idea he's getting sent to the mall. I was going to tell him, but figured it'll be more fun to watch his reaction."

"You're an evil bastard... probably why I like you."

The trio fell silent as they watched Ann visit each of the cars, engaging them through open driver side windows.

"So, what's she saying?" Randy asked.

"My guess, she's trying to talk some of them into staying. I say good riddance. Probably a bunch of pseudo-intellectual pricks I didn't like."

"Well, boys, I gotta mount up." Finn turned to leave, responding to the revving engines of the impatient caravan.

"Yo, Helpful, before you go, you mentioned talking to FOB Olmsted about your family and Stan. So, tell me, how often do you talk to them?"

Randy's muffled laugh tilted Finn's head suspiciously. "Twice a day. Why?"

"Well, seems to me we didn't get the hardware you promised."

Finn waited for Abe to finish, but after several ticks, he realized Abe wasn't offering anything else. "Spit it out, *Willings*. I don't have all day."

"I'm shocked you didn't stack the blocks. Seriously, the better I get to know you, the more concerned I become with your intellectual capacity."

"For the love of God, spit it *out!*"

"Stuff, Sergeant Helpful, ask them for stuff. We need more equipment. We didn't scavenge nearly enough from the aid center and we need a ton. You know, the stuff my tax dollars bought. Tell one of your friends to have it fall off the back of a truck, or whatever you military guys call it. If it's bothering you, just think of it this way. You're simply reassigning it to its rightful owner!"

"*Owners.*"

"Thank you, Randy — *owners*. Because, if I'm... we're joining a scavenging team or the strike team, we need the proper equipment for the job."

"I'll take your request under advisement. Until then, keep your gun clean and your reloading press in proper working order."

"So, no?"

"I'll touch base when we get back. And don't stay up all night worrying your pearls. We start training tomorrow, crack of dawn. Get some rest. You'll need it."

Abe and Randy watched as Finn jogged to a waiting Humvee.

"He's not bringing anything back, is he?"

"Nope."

# Chapter 5

Blum rattled awake. The stench — the earthy chemical stench, tinged with rot — had wrenched him from a deep sleep. His senses came online slowly as he stared at the moon through the open second-story window.

He strained to clear the sleep from his mind. Was the stench simply a lingering fragment of a nightmare or the terrifying result of air permeated with rotting particulate?

"Shit!" It was real, and unbearably strong.

How long had he been asleep? His body told him only minutes. A glance at his Bertucci DX3 wristwatch revealed the truth — three hours. He'd slept through his two-hour security check. "Damn it!" He feared this would happen. He'd let himself get too comfortable in the apartment he'd commandeered in Haven. His plan for an overnight rest after he'd refueled his Humvee turned into a weeklong respite upon discovering the town was abandoned and its only diner heavily stocked with canned goods and whiskey. Haven had held true to its name. Now he was staring into complacency's cold, unforgiving eyes.

With slow, deliberate movements, Blum slinked from the bed and slid his feet into his Danners. They were the only clothing he removed while sleeping and the current situation was the reason why.

A quick glance at his kit confirmed it was where he'd left it — at the end of the bed, next to his M4. With feathery steps, he crept toward the window. A slight breeze rustled the threadbare drapes and carried with it the noxious odor that had rousted him from his slumber. It also removed all doubt... the infected had found his sanctuary. Now, he needed to recon their force size.

A yard from the window, Blum dropped to his knees and crawled to the sill. He was confident he'd remain undetected, with the downwind breeze masking his scent, but still advanced excruciatingly slow.

A chorus of arid rasps rode the putrid stench as his eyes crested the sill. He would have gasped if he wasn't holding his breath. The cloudless night bathed the infected in crystal-blue light and made apparent their overwhelming numbers.

*What the... where did you come from?* His thought interrupted as his stinging eyes followed their marching ranks down Main Street. Dozens of them.

Blum had chosen this apartment, on the corner of Berwick and Main, for its tactical position. It afforded him an unobstructed view of two enemy approach routes, and was on the corner of the primary thoroughfare into Haven. He'd parked the Humvee, stocked with provisions and a little bit of whiskey, directly under the aging apartment's southern windows, facing west on Berwick, with the assumption the threat would approach from the east, using Route 940, which transitioned to Berwick at the Lehigh River overpass. The narrow bridge would bottleneck the enemy and provide clear lines of fire. His assumption was correct, and had he been awake when they arrived, his strategy would have paid dividends. As it stood, he'd trapped himself.

Blum brought his view back to the infected at his doorstep. They seemed focused, or as focused as their limited brain function would allow, on continuing west, the same direction as his home.

"Son of a..." he whispered — an infected had stopped and arched his head. Blum slid from the window. He'd seen that before. His scent was in the wind, and the infected had latched on. He duckwalked to the room's center point, stood, and rushed to his kit.

Geared up in a flash, he spun a slow circle. The defenses he'd developed, although meager, were still in place and would slow the infected when they breached the door. Glass shattering on the first floor signaled the time for stealth had passed.

"Follow your plan," he whispered as he knelt behind the upended kitchen table positioned in front of the living room window, its peeling sheet-plastic surface facing the apartment's only entrance. The three rooms of the tiny apartment offered him no defensible fallback position. The window, with a ten-foot drop to the hood of his Humvee, was his only option. His M4 no sooner came to rest on the table's edge, when the monsters arrived — this was it, time to fight.

Bangs and shaking were what he'd expected. Instead, the doorknob rattled. "It's locked, you stupid bastards!" His shouted taunt spurred the infected forward, causing the door to creak under their surge.

The tubular steel-framed chair wedged under the doorknob wouldn't hold long once they forced the door open. He knew this as fact. But it would slow them and hopefully funnel them to the left, where he'd set a series of tripwires and had moved the apartment's heavier furniture to act as directional obstructions. Combined, it would buy him about sixty seconds.

None of his defenses would kill, and that wasn't their purpose. He needed to draw the infected into the building, crowd them together on the tight staircase, and launch his counteroffensive.

A putrid, yet cooling, breeze across his damp neck sent gooseflesh down his spine and reminded him the threat was everywhere. He chanced a glimpse out the window — the horde had closed ranks, with most of them fighting their way into the building to join their brethren in the hunt.

A sharp crack spun Blum's focus back to the door. Its frame was failing. "Come on... I'm waiting! Bet I taste like steak — rare and warm."

Blum ducked behind the table as fissures raced down the wall surrounding the door. This wasn't going as planned.

"Adapt and overcome!" Blum popped up from behind the table and sent half a dozen rounds into the splintering wall, adjusted his aim, and dumped the rest of his magazine into the door.

On his feet, he swapped magazines and watched as the wall flexed, appearing to breathe. How many infected were in the hallway? How many more could fit?

The groan of wood strained to its limits unlocked Blum's legs, and he spun to face the window. The stragglers were fixated on entering the building, just as he'd hoped. An instant later, the wall succumbed to the force of dozens of ravenous bodies and exploded.

Blum flinched as drywall and shards of destroyed framing rained on his back. He pivoted to face the mass. "Kiss my ass, you nasty maggots!" His M4 spit three-round-bursts into shins and thighs, but there were too many bodies. He'd run out of time!

With his battle rifle strapped tight across his chest, he backed through the window as the infected slid through and trampled their downed comrades. His fingertips flared white as they clung to the narrow sill, his body dangling feet from his waiting Humvee. Coarse fingers clawed at his grip. It was the motivation he needed to freefall to safety.

The bricks of the building's facade rushing through his vision ended when his left foot landed atop one of the Humvees hood-mounted airlift hooks. It folded under his weight and ricocheted his body into the windshield. A pained yelp caught in his throat as he pushed off the windshield and glanced over the war wagon's hardtop to the street behind. A figure standing twenty yards away, maybe less, had locked its black eyes on him.

Were his eyes playing tricks? "You!" Blum shouted as he finished pushing his frame to its full height, then toppled backwards, landing hard on his kitbag. He was hurt, not incapacitated, but definitely in trouble. His ankle couldn't support his weight, but had to!

"Embrace the suck!" he shouted as he rolled from the hood. His right leg buckled, but didn't fail, and held his balance as his head swiveled back and forth, searching for threats.

Blum jolted as skin slapped against concrete behind him. With his left foot suspended like a gimped dog's paw, he twisted toward the sound when an infected suddenly thumped to the hood of the Humvee. The same airlift hook that had ruined his ankle now protruded through the monster's emaciated ribcage.

"Well, look at you, ya ghoulish shit."

Another body bounced off the pavement and snapped him from his stupor. He glanced up. They were hurling themselves through the window. Three bounding, one-legged hops and a slap of the door latch delivered him into the relative safety of the Humvee. But he wasn't retreating, not yet.

With the steering wheel cranked hard left, he gunned the V8 and went on the offensive. The Humvee rocked on its springs as it bounced over the curb, tossing the infected from its hood, and leveled off facing the bearded man.

\*\*\*

Sampson's head bowed, shielding his eyes from the stinging lights of the fighter's machine. *This fighter should be easy to defeat.* He thought in response to the machine's roaring engine, but lack of movement. *He focuses only on me, his surroundings blocked by the tunnel he stares through.*

Sampson fought the blinding light and jutted his chin at the machine, his taunt meant to goad the fighter to act. When the steady roar pitched to a near scream, Sampson smiled. The machine would cover the distance in a matter of seconds.

As the glaring lights dominated his vision, Sampson lunged right, tossing his body to the pavement and rolling from the machine's path. The fire hydrant that his body had hidden now waited to end the machine and trap the meat inside — defenseless.

A hissing mist coated Sampson as he rolled into a predatory crouch, then launched his body toward the fountain of water gushing from the fractured hydrant. He spun frantically; searching for the disabled machine when brake lights in the distance signaled his failure.

***

Blum held his tenuous grip on the steering wheel as the Humvee fishtailed through the street. The brush guard's glancing impact against the cast iron hydrant had nearly ripped it free of his control as the vehicle pitched and shuddered violently.

Blum punched the dashboard. He'd had the chance to end the monster in Central Park, but his humanity had caused him to hesitate. Now the walking atrocity roamed free. How many lives had this monster taken because of his mistake? "Never again!"

His ankle throbbed as he resisted the urge to circle back and finish the abomination — it would only waste time and fuel. His stay in Haven had ended; it was time to go home.

# Chapter 6

"Sergeant Finn! I believe you bear the responsibility to escort us to the refugee camp. Our safe arrival rests on your shoulders. Please form up, or whatever you military types call it."

Finn's features pinched. Stanley's tone held a hard edge, harder than a man in his position should attempt. "Stanley, I'm telling you for the last time. You're on your own. We have business to attend to here. The FEMA center is about thirty minutes away. You should be fine. Just stay on main roads... if you can."

Stanley surged toward Finn — the sergeant didn't flinch. "We were closer to the FEMA center when we left the community. This is relevant, as I suspect you received advanced notice we would be turned away from this military installation. You are now responsible for our protection until we arrive at the intake center. Have I made myself clear?"

Finn leaned in, now mere inches from Stanley's face. He smirked as sweat bubbled from the man's forehead. "You should've been executed for what you did. I begged Ann to sentence you to death and volunteered to pull the trigger. So, Stanley, ask yourself how safe you actually are in my presence."

"Your preposterous behavior is merely a ruse designed to elicit our exit. You don't intimidate us. I've battled thugs and bullies my entire life and in the end you're all cut from the same cowardly cloth which sends you running..."

Stanley slapped at Finn's hand, but the Sergeant's choking grip was too powerful. He clawed for the man's eyes, attempting to scratch them out, just to be lifted into the air and tossed like a rag doll against his idling car.

"You have thirty seconds to leave. At thirty-one, I kill you." Finn spun to face the gate. A grin blossomed when a car door slammed. Stanley's caravan was pulling away a moment later.

*\*\*\**

The instant he exited the inspection center, Finn beelined for the information hub. Their families would arrive at the gate in thirty minutes, but he had something to do before rejoining his team. The soldier at the info hub was hesitant to help, but relented after being told the reason and made Finn promise not to tell anyone. *An easy promise to keep.*

Now, he stood at the entrance, searching for the nerve to see this through. He owed it to his team. He reached into his breast pocket and stroked the cold steel it held. Funny, he'd envisioned this moment hundreds of times, knew exactly what he wanted to do, and how to do it. But standing at the JWSOF shelter's threshold robbed him of his courage. He'd need every ounce to get through this.

With a cut glance skyward, Finn pounded on the shelter's wooden frame. It took a while, but a frail woman with hollow eyes finally pulled the canvas door open. "Hey, Finn. I just put Robby down. If you don't mind, I'm going to let him sleep."

Finn nodded and waited, but Amber didn't ask him in. "What can I do for you?"

"You're sure you don't want to join us, Amber? It's not perfect, but we're working on it. Robby would have other kids to play with and front yards to play in."

Amber just stared at him, her expression unreadable, but Finn knew she blamed him for Jones' death. "I'm sorry; I'll be on my way. But I have something for you." She flinched as he reached into his breast pocket. Why, he didn't know.

He held out his hand and waited. When she didn't move, or acknowledge his action, he unfurled the ball chain and quickly looped it over her head, guiding it around her neck. "Allen would have wanted you to have these," he said as the dog tags came to rest. "Make sure Robby knows his dad was a hero." Finn's voice cracked as he struggled to finish. "If you need anything, ask the radio room to reach out to me."

Amber's lips quivered as her hand squeezed her husband's tags. She shut the door with a slight nod and left Finn alone with his guilt.

*** 

The Sergeant watched his men reunite with their families and smiled. Happy squeals from little ones joined the quiet sobs of husbands and wives embracing for the first time in over two weeks.

"I'll be damned, Shamus Finn — it's about time!"

Finn spun towards the voice. "Aislin Finn, I'm surprised you're not in the brig."

"Being related to the great Sergeant Finn comes with perks." Aislin dropped her lone bag and charged Finn, wrapped him in a tight hug, and whispered, "Thank you for getting me out of this place!"

Finn pulled back and stared at his only living relative. Breaking tradition, his genuinely Irish family had produced only two children. Finn's brother, Caden, had died shortly after Aislin's mother lost her battle with cancer. Finn was convinced that Caden's broken heart had killed him. His death certificate called it heart failure, one and the same as far as he was concerned.

With no other living family, and even if there were, Finn had jumped at the chance to raise the young girl, adopting her two weeks after Caden's death. His brother never asked it of him, because he knew he didn't have to — he died knowing Finn would take care of Aislin.

It had happened shortly after his last active duty deployment, and a month before his next. He scrambled to transition to full-time National Guard status and did so with the help of some of the finest people he'd ever met. It meant giving up some of his military aspirations, and an eight-year career defined by exemplary service. But both had become unexpectedly insignificant. Seven years had passed since their first days together as a family unit. And he wouldn't have traded a second of it.

"You look more like your dad every day."

"And you look more like grandma every day!"

Finn pulled Aislin in for another hug. Her sharp comeback told him she had weathered her time in the camp like the rock he knew she was.

"Tell me about our new place," she queried, as they parted and she went to retrieve her bag.

"It's a neighborhood, an actual house in a neighborhood. You'll have your own room with an attached bathroom. I've seen a few women your age, but all the boys are eunuchs, or will be soon. I know, rough break."

"My own bathroom! Holy shi... *wait*, what's the catch?" Aislin ignored his eunuch crack. She'd heard it for years, as had every date brave enough to meet her adoptive father. It was usually a first date / last date situation.

"It's all just starting to gel, but you'll be put to work. We've got crews working on securing our perimeter, trying to get a security team built, crops planted, and you'll be helping. Also, we have a young girl, a refugee of sorts, that I'd like you to spend some time with. She's been through a lot and needs a friend closer to her own age. Oh, and there's a guy. His name's *Abel Andrew Willings*. He's the guy I told you about after the parking garage incident, well, him and his motley crew. Try to ignore him. It's not easy, but try."

Aislin's brow cocked. "Is he *able and willing* to accept us?"

"Ha, he's also sensitive about his name. Probably why he'll forget yours directly after you're introduced. He's actually looking forward to having a fresh injection of people. If not for him, you'd be bunking in this camp indefinitely. I only brought him up because... well, he's a bit *much*. You'll see."

Aislin held Finn's stare without further comment, but her mischievous grin spoke volumes.

"What?"

"Oh, just wondering about your green-eyed lady. You know, the one you babbled on about after you saved her from the parking garage. And then every single time we talked."

"Yes, Aislin, you'll meet Nic. She's looking forward to it... please be nice."

"When have I not been nice?" she asked, feigning insult. "I'm downright effervescent. Buuut, I recall several instances where respectable young men were driven from our apartment in tears after meeting you. I've always appreciated the tactics you employ; they saved me from many a heartache. So, I'm sure you'll embrace my taking the same approach to ensure your happiness."

"Load up with the others," Finn said, pinching the bridge of his nose while regretting telling her about Nic. "I have to talk to the CO about supplies." He spun, looking for his team. "Donovan, I've got some business with the CO. Pack everyone up. I'll be back in ten."

Donovan acknowledged Finn's order with a beaming smile and his wife nestled under his arm. "You heard the man. Let's pack up and go *home!*"

## Chapter 7

Stanley's caravan limped to the first swing barrier twenty-five yards from the FEMA refugee center's main gate. It wasn't what he'd envisioned. The converted mall had been, to the best of his recollection, an upscale retail hub.

"Crystal, is this how you remember the mall?"

"No, and that was a foolish question. We're not going shopping, Stanley. We're refugees. What did you expect to find, manicured green spaces with people frolicking about celebrating the end of the world?"

Her venomous reply clearly signaled she'd not come to terms with their being exiled. "I suppose you have a valid point, although a less caustic tone to convey your observation would be appreciated."

"And you... you could have not been the pseudo-intellectual ass who willfully invited monsters into our neighborhood. Now, you *will* go to the gate, talk to the soldiers, explain that *you are* responsible for all the people you talked into leaving with us, and make arrangements for our entry!"

Stanley's mouth slacked open as he stared at Crystal. Her hard truth cut deep and stifled his reply as he unlatched the door and slid from the car.

Ignoring the signs warning refugees to remain in their vehicles, he crept under the lift-barrier and walked toward the main double gate. He was vaguely aware of the soldiers in armored vehicles and guard towers monitoring his approach. But his focus was drawn to the sea of canvas shelters covering the FEMA center's parking lot. Literally hundreds of them. *How many more are housed within the building's interior?*

"Stop!" a mechanically amplified voice ordered.

He registered the command, but it seemed far away as he watched people scurry through tight aisles between shelters.

"We will employ lethal force if you continue your approach!"

*Someone's in trouble,* his thought was distant as his eyes followed a line of refugees, holding silver trays, to an enormous tent with large metal vents protruding through its roof.

"Warning shot!"

Stanley recoiled, stutter-stepped, and searched for cover with his head buried in the crooks of his elbows as the bullet blistered the pavement and sprayed his shins with stinging asphalt.

"Do we have your attention?"

Stanley nodded, his arms still covering his head, and hollered a muffled, "Yes!"

"Good. State your intentions."

"We seek safe harbor behind your well-defended fencing. Our community, uh, uh failed! It was overrun due to poor leadership."

"Is your name Stanley Chatham traveling with wife, Crystal?"

Stanley yanked his head free of its protective cover and searched with wild eyes for the man speaking to him. "Sir, please identify yourself and offer an elucidation as to your knowledge of my name."

"Dunn, what the hell does elucidation mean?" Private Sanderson asked.

Corporal Dunn rubbed his temples. "It means Finn was right — another pompous dickweed has arrived at our gate."

"Sir, I demand..."

"Stanley, you're in no position to demand a damn thing," Dunn growled, mustering every ounce of his self-control. "Follow my directions, and we won't shoot you. Move to the inspection tent. You'll know it by the sign, written in large red letters, which spell, *inspection tent*. If you can't read, which appears likely, look for the big red cross. Enter, disrobe, and sit down. A medical technician will inspect you for signs of infection. If you clear inspection, a soldier will escort you to my position, at which point I will give you a sheet of paper. On said paper are the rules, regulations, and instructions for entering and becoming a resident of this facility. You'll be granted an opportunity to review this information with your fellow refugees. Have I been clear?"

Stanley scowled at the young soldier with the bullhorn. "I'm capable of interpreting the written word. Advise your medical team I will arrive momentarily. I anticipate a proficient and timely procedure and look forward to making your acquaintance in the same comportment."

"Sanderson, be prepared to shoot this one."

\*\*\*

"I find these rules to be tyrannically restrictive. They seem to have been written for an inmate population. Wouldn't you agree, Sergeant? Also, you've failed to answer my inquiry about your advanced knowledge of our arrival."

"You're free to seek shelter elsewhere. As for your *inquiry*, bite me. Anything else?"

"You, good sir, are a public servant. Speaking to a member of the public in..."

"And you, ya pompous windbag, are a liar. Your community was attacked, but survived. If the information I received from Sergeant Finn is accurate, and I have no reason to believe it isn't, it was your fault. Now, I've supplied you the rules. Are you officially requesting refugee status on behalf of yourself and your group?"

Stanley glanced at the small caravan. His followers were waiting outside their vehicles, stretching stiff backs and staring at him expectantly. "I recall you offered me the opportunity to discuss our options with the persons in my procession. Does your offer still stand?"

"You have fifteen minutes. Your presence outside the gate will draw infected to our location. I can't allow that to happen."

\*\*\*

Stanley glanced around the area as the gate behind him locked shut. He imagined this was the way caged zoo animals viewed the world. He balled the RRI list and shoved it deep into his pocket as the gate in front of him, the second of the double entry gate system, slid open, freeing him from the main gate enclosure.

"They have denied us entry," he lied, with his chin jutted defiantly. "It seems Sergeant Finn has misrepresented the facts surrounding our expulsion. I'm certain his intent was to ensure the death penalty he enthusiastically supported, be carried out by the monsters roaming our city."

His followers bristled as their predicament crystallized. "Now, now, don't fret. I have another location in mind. One which affords us a combination of safety and freedom."

His back stiffened as the caravan's anxiety seemed to lift. He'd always fancied himself a superior orator, and his command of this group bolstered his belief. But as he searched their faces, sharing a confident nod with each member as their eyes locked, he noticed Crystal was missing. Stanley peered over the shoulders of his gathered faction and found his wife seated in their car with her face buried in her hands.

Stanley's lips twisted into a sneer. Maybe it was finally time to rid himself of the asphyxiating shrew?

## Chapter 8

Sampson spurred his soldiers forward, towards the wreckage of the small city. Its name unimportant, he focused on the movement at its center.

A familiar scent permeated the air. Familiar, yes, but different from that of his soldiers or their food. They'd encountered and enlisted others like his soldiers as they marched in search of fresh hunting grounds. But these were not of his ilk.

*The tentacles of the one called Su have reached far,* he realized as he watched The Others scurry through the shadow cast by a large glass and steel building. It was them, the weak ones, afraid of the sun even as it hung low in the sky.

What drew them to that building when there were dozens of structures for them to cool their fragile skin? What drove them into the stinging light? A reptilian grin cracked through the muck covering his cheeks. *They seek food.*

Sampson's pace quickened, then faltered as the thick, cooling air vibrated. Soft at first, it quickly turned violent as a machine burst from a low cloud and circled above his soldiers.

\*\*\*

Captain Archer pulled the Bell 407GX into a circling hover. "Big Blue for base."

"What'cha got, Big Blue?"

"A problem. I've got eyes on at least a thousand infected en route to our front door and moving with purpose."

"Repeat force size!"

"At least one thousand. I say again, at least one thousand infected heading toward base."

"Bring it in, Big Blue. We're scrambling QRF teams now. If they join forces with the infected harassing our main entrance... arm yourself upon touchdown."

Archer pulled the bird out of its drift and pushed the Allison Turboshaft power plant to full throttle. "Base, ready two gunners. Get them to the landing pad, pronto. We have to blunt their advance. We already have enough problems and won't be able to hold them off if they link up with the infected already on site."

The Bell 407GX wasn't a war bird, but its airframe, built for life flight service, was stable and tough. It would easily handle the weight of the gunners and their ammunition. But it lacked gun mounts. The soldiers would be forced to either fire from the prone position or trust the bird's retention lanyards and lean out with twenty-seven-pound M240 machineguns trying to pull them to their deaths. A quick rundown of the Bell's interior, mechanics, and lack of a metal safety plating between him and very deadly weapons, helped him decide. They'd have to trust the lanyards. He was the only pilot they had. Going tits up meant a lot of sick people died.

"Big Blue, gunners en route." After an uneasy pause, his point of contact continued. "Archer, I know what you're planning — you sure about this? One of those yahoos goes sideways and puts a round through the roof and your hero move goes Charlie Foxtrot double quick."

"Thanks for the positive vibes, Smitty. Get them to the roof A-SAP."

"How's your fuel?"

"I'm yellow on fuel. But we don't have time to top off. Our operating zone will be close enough that I'll be skids down before Bitchin' Betty warns me on fuel."

Archer glanced at his fuel gage and its adjacent warning light. Bitchin Betty, the voice that would alert him to an emergency, would come on long before they thinned the infected adequately. He dismissed the thought. He'd been here before. It was part of the game, and he planned on winning.

\*\*\*

The bearded monster disappeared as Blum set his binoculars on the rough aggregate surface of the office building's roof. It was him, the infected who'd laid a near fatal trap in Haven. "This can't be happening," he mumbled. He'd escaped this mob thirty-six hours ago. They couldn't have caught up to him already. "I guess that's what happens when you never sleep."

His ankle throbbed as he kneeled behind the parapet and watched the life flight copter break from its circling pattern above the horde and blaze towards the hospital.

Its return flight was happening the exact time as it had yesterday. It departed into the eastern sky three hours earlier and returned from the west, in what Blum guessed was a Groundhog Day type cadence.

His view of the hospital complex, roughly two miles east of his position, and its primary approach was unobstructed. It's why he chose this roost to observe the hospital before attempting to navigate the infected surrounding its entrance.

All he wanted was some Motrin, or any anti-inflammatory, actually — and some ice. The drug stores he'd raided had long ago been ransacked. He needed to get into the hospital before his ankle swelled further. Already afraid to remove his boot, worried he'd never get it back on, Blum understood what would happen if he didn't get the swelling under control.

He'd tried to signal the helicopter yesterday, but its sudden appearance left him mere seconds to react. It was a mile past him by the time he'd struggled to his feet and started waving his arms. Today, though, he was prepared because he was determined not to spend another night on the roof.

Blum glanced to the copious amounts of debris he'd gathered from the sharp corners of the roof's parapet. Brittle twigs, dead leaves, and scraps of windblown paper would have provided ample fuel for the gunpowder to ignite a smoldering signal fire. Now, however, he was down a round of 5.56 ammo and watching the helicopter land on the hospital's rooftop helipad. All because he'd lost his situational awareness while tracking his nemesis. *That son of a bitch is determined to kill me one way or another.*

Sliding behind the low wall, he sneered as his hand went to his helmet and again found his headset's destroyed boom mic. He wasn't sure how, or even when, it happened because he hadn't given it two thoughts since escaping Central Park. If it were operational, a quick scan of the channels, and he'd be talking to the soldiers in the hospital and, shortly after, waiting for the bird to scoop him up.

The heavy thump of helicopter rotors under strain reached him an instant before the beautiful sound of M240's rattling to life pierced the dusky night.

*** 

Sampson's focus remained on the enemy, his soldiers falling away, mutilated by the fighter's weapons, held little importance. He'd soon replenish his ranks. Su's breed, however, could not be allowed to stand.

The ground at his feet exploded, but still he charged the blight who dared to deprive his soldiers of the food they craved — that he craved.

Static scrambled his mind as his soldiers fell in greater numbers. The fighter's weapons were churning through them as The Others watched on from the cool comfort of the building's shade. His soldiers had become nearly unreachable, but their instinct to feed ensured they'd follow him and whatever action he took. That was all he needed.

Yards from the enemy, he risked a glance over his shoulder; the fighter's weapons had halved his army. But they would still overwhelm The Others.

Mere feet from the shadow's edge, Sampson slowed his soldiers to a crawl. His head tilted in question as the enemy formed into a straight line, preparing to fight. A raspy chuckle escaped his gullet as he darted into their battle line and seized the head of the closest enemy.

The snap of vertebrae pulsed through his arms and sent his soldiers into a violent frenzy. The din of battle quickly rose as more of his soldiers entered the fray and easily masked the grind of metal and sputtering roar above them.

\*\*\*

"Shut up!" Captain Archer spat as he struggled against the *Cyclic* and slammed the *Collective* down. Betty was screeching multiple warnings, but the hydraulic system failure was the warning he was fighting to overcome.

"Grounds coming up fast, Captain," one of the unseen gunners warned.

"Get inside and brace. We're going to hit hard." Hovering at two hundred feet when the mission went sideways, Archer had seconds to regain control of the crippled bird and execute an emergency landing. They'd pushed the copter too hard for too long, and it just voiced its displeasure by spitting shrapnel through the hydraulic lines.

Archer's biceps screamed as he pulled back on the *Cyclic* to pitch the copter's nose up and slow their descent. If he could do that, they'd still slam to the pavement, but wouldn't break apart. If the bird lost structural integrity, the fuel tank would rupture and they'd most likely die in the ensuing inferno.

"Boys, if you believe in God, *now* would be the time to ask Him for a favor," he yelled as he lowered his head and pulled with every muscle in his body. Something in his low back rolled under the strain, sending bolts of pain down his legs, but still he pulled back on the *Cyclic*.

The sensation of tilting skyward jolted his head upright. His relief twisted to dread as they leveled off and the hospital's glass facade filled the bird's windscreen. "Cover..."

A rotor blade slicing through glass and steel ended Archer's warning. Shards of severed carbon fiber rifled through the cargo hold's open doors as the copter slammed to the pavement then twisted viciously to the left.

Archer ducked behind the instrument panel a flash before remnants of crumpled steel framing crashed through the windscreen. His body shuddered brutally as the Allison Turboshaft fought to free ruined rotor blades from the fissure they'd created in the hospital's facade. With the last of its out-of-control thrust, the power plant pulled the tail boom through the jagged hole, ripping it from the airframe and hurling it across the lobby, where it slashed through the military's barricade. It was the hospital's last line of defense against the infected.

## The Wild Ones

Gunfire pierced the ringing in his ears as he struggled to free his legs from beneath the ruined flight control panel. Archer knew what it meant. He had to escape or the infected would devour him.

"Little help!"

Neither gunner responded. He didn't ask again. Blood dripping onto his shoulder told him they wouldn't answer. High velocity debris had shattered them.

Smoke carried noxious fumes to the cockpit, increasing Archer's struggle to free his legs. With grinding teeth, he forced them to the right while jagged steel ripped into his flight suit and clawed through his skin. He'd pay for it — if he survived.

Heat pulsed through the cockpit as his hand slammed down on the latch, but the jammed crew door held fast. Again his hand worked the latch, again it refused to respond. Through blurred eyes, he searched for the jettison lever, then slid his hand to the floor and grasped it just before his lungs rebelled against the lethal fumes. At the edge of consciousness, he yanked the lever up and gulped fresh air as the crew door spiraled to the ground.

Archer slid from the cockpit and doubled over, retching smoke and fumes from his lungs. As he hacked what he was sure was half of his left lung to the pavement, dozens of rounds blistered the surrounding air. Their targets became clear as he stood as straight as the spasm in his lower back would allow.

Infected, blurred by stinging eyes, roamed the area in numbers he'd never seen while countless others lay broken and scattered. Instinct to put steel between him and the monsters drove him toward the helicopter's open bay door — but flames and remnants of his gunners repelled him and left him searching for an escape route.

With the copter's wreckage between him and the hospital, Archer understood how exposed he was and that he faced two horrifying choices: dart for the hospital entrance and pray the soldiers within recognized he wasn't simply another infected, or navigate the surging monsters and seek shelter behind one of the many vehicles abandoned in the hospital's parking lot.

His vision clearing, he searched for a route through the infected. His head tilted as two realities clashed with logic. Pockets of infected seemed to be... fighting, actually locked in mortal combat. He'd never seen this happen, nor was it covered in any of the intelligence briefings. In those meetings, they were told the infected excelled at cooperative hunting. This was anything but cooperative. The second aberration — he hadn't been attacked. While most of the infected not engaged in the melee rushed the hospital's jagged breach, others formed a semi-circle around him and the flaming copter, but held their ground at ten yards. "You're afraid of fire... you can *reason!*"

A ripple swept through the black-eyed mob as one of them darted forward, then retreated. Archer staggered back to escape the mock attack and stumbled when his heel tangled with something heavy. Inches from tumbling into the burning cargo hold, he threw his body forward and twisted to the pavement.

"Son of a bitch," he shouted, as pain radiated from his lower back and swallowed every inch of his body.

The struggle to right himself and the bellowed outburst ignited a flame in the infected. They inched forward like hyenas isolating a wounded gazelle. Their willingness to brave the heat in exchange for Archer's flesh grew as they trundled closer. On his knees, he bit back the pain and searched for a weapon. Eyes on the hesitant mob, his hands scrabbled along the pavement. A bolt of hope punched through his gut when his right hand brushed against the object that had caused him to fall. He only hoped its ammo pouch held enough rounds to stop the mob's creeping advance.

Archer nearly toppled when he tugged on the machinegun, but quickly righted himself and heaved the weapon to his shoulder and sent a short burst into the center of his enemy's line.

He focused on their legs, as he'd been trained, and toppled half a dozen infected, but the line's edges continued their march. Archer shuffled back, getting as close to the flames as his sizzling skin would allow.

The gunfire within the hospital ceased — Archer was alone. "Kiss my ass, ya freaks! You're all coming with me!" Struggling to his feet, he unleashed the machinegun's power. Its full-throated roar led his charge at the infected as they crumpled under the barrage.

Feet from their line, the infected countered his charge; many sacrificed themselves so others could eat. This was the cooperative hunting he'd been briefed on and it would prove lethally effective.

Archer swept through their ranks one last time, then focused on thinning their left flank. This game wasn't over and he was playing to win. Steps from contact, the M240 sent its last round downrange, but twenty-seven pounds of steel, in the right hands, was still a formidable weapon.

He waited until he could see the dying sunlight glint off their black eyes, then spun a tight circle. The jolt of metal splintering infected skulls nearly wrenched the gun from his extended hands as the follow through dragged him several stumbling feet to the left.

He pivoted, raised the weapon above his head, and froze.

"Great pose, but you should get in!"

Archer charged to the Humvee with the M240 still whirling above his head. He hadn't heard the war machine approach, but that didn't matter. He was going to live!

# Chapter 9

Abe watched sweat drip from his nose and splash into the growing puddle on the pavement. Elbows on his knees, and his head resting on crossed forearms, the puddle between his feet became his singular focus.

"I can't believe you didn't tell us you had a daughter, or niece, or whatever the hell she is. I'm hurt, man. I thought we were friends, but now you're a stranger to me."

"I knew. I figured you did, too."

Abe lifted his head and glared at Randy, snorted, and dropped it back on his forearms.

"So, Stone. Did you know?"

"I think we need some water. It's a hot one and we've been pushing hard."

"Nice deflection. I expect it from Randy... but my own brother? That's cold, just cold."

"I knew! Lu knows, too."

Abe lifted his head and swatted at his ear. "Did you guys hear that? I think we're infested with those annoying little gnats. I'll bring Raid with me tomorrow."

Nic scoffed her distain, but Finn stifled her retort with a stealthy shake of his head in a quiet plea to bring the temperature down.

"Gage, you're awfully quiet. Infected got your tongue?"

Gage flinched. "Look, Abe, I, I just, you know, go with the flow. No harm no foul, mind my own business and all that."

"Longest non-answer to a yes or no question I've ever heard, Gage." Abe put his head down again. "Everyone I know is a jackass."

The group sat in awkward silence as the mid-day sun blazed overhead. Finn had pulled them together when he returned last night and laid out his plan. This group, under Finn's command, had become Strike Team Alpha. Robins, Donovan, and Billings had been split off to bring various other teams together. He hadn't offered the community a reason for the abrupt change in force structure, other than to say he was honoring his commitment to train them and determined this was the best structure. Military efficiency was what he'd called it.

His hand brushed against his breast pocket, then fell away. It wasn't the time, especially with Abe's present *condition*. He needed them focused on training. Their minds churning through imaginary missions was exactly what he wanted to avoid.

"So, Sergeant Helpful *Stranger*, what's the word on supplies? I assume you're planning on getting us more than helmets, gloves, and headsets?" Abe tapped a gloved hand to his helmeted head for emphasis.

Finn grimaced. "Hey, we secured a cargo truck's worth of food, too. Give me some credit."

"Got food — need military equipment."

"You've got food. A lot of our community doesn't. So, there's *that*. The radios will prove invaluable outside the wire. The helmets might keep that thick skull of yours from getting dinged. Which, I'm sure you'll agree, would only add to your intellectual deficiencies."

"Insulting my intellect... how original. You've cut me to my core. I may never recover." Abe's dry tone matched his expressionless stare.

"Ladies and gentlemen, boys and girls, this concludes our afternoon bitch session. On your feet and stack up. We're clearing this house again." Finn ordered, abruptly ending the back and forth with Abe.

Groans and mumbled expletives greeted Finn as his weary team struggled to their feet. He nodded as they stood; they still had fight in them.

He dropped back during their sluggish approach and regarded the house. It was the only one left unoccupied after Ann assigned his team and their families' permanent living quarters. She let them skip quarantine, reasoning their time on a military base ensured they arrived free of infection.

He'd spent a good portion of the evening fashioning musty cardboard boxes into faux adversaries and positioned them throughout the structure's interior. Between each run-through, he moved them to different locations. His team was tasked with clearing the home as a squad, then individually. They had three seconds to react to the enemy or they were deemed killed in action and forced to run a lap around the community. Abe had managed six laps, but attributed his poor performance to the fact they were dry firing at the cardboard cutouts. He insisted he'd hold the top score if not for that simple detail.

"What aren't you telling us?"

Finn stutter stepped away from the whispered voice, then realized it was coming through his headset. "We're radio silent until we enter the structure, Abe. You're begging to run more laps."

"Can the BS. You tossed us into hardcore door-to-door combat training on day one. Plus, when we talked about forming strike teams, it was to neutralize infected threats approaching the community. I believe your exact words were *we won't search for trouble, just defend what's ours*."

Finn's lips pulled tight exposing gnashing teeth. He knew Strike Team Alpha would go rigid and change their approach to training if he briefed them now.

"Meet at my house tonight after Nic gets home from guard duty. Don't tell her where you're going. And, Abe, keep your mouth shut."

"I don't know if I can do that, Helpful Stranger. The more laps I run, the more delirious I get. Next thing you know, my gums start bumping and I'm spreading rumors. Then, all kinds of ugly breaks out."

Finn couldn't contain his chuckle. This guy was always and forever working an angle. "You have four seconds to react. Oh, and you really are a prick."

"Please, I'm a flipping ray of sunshine. I'll see you tonight."

# Chapter 10

Blum followed his passenger's directions and pulled the Humvee into a sharp left turn, then stood on the accelerator.

"Jay Blum," he shouted over the roaring engine.

"Chuck Archer. Thanks for pulling my ass out of the fire. Go right, follow route eleven to Continental, then straight-line to the river."

"Do you have any Motrin?" Blum asked, as he wheeled onto R11.

Archer's face strained. "Did you ask me for a Motrin?"

"So, I take it, you don't. Any idea where I can find some?" He bumped onto Continental and raced toward the Susquehanna River, then glanced at Archer.

Archer's mouth moved in silent answer. His mind caught in a loop of rattling off the countless stores where America's favorite painkiller could be found and remembering the world had died, and with it, society's easy access to everything.

"Are you regular army or one of those militia we've been seeing along the Pike?" he asked, breaking from his stupor.

"Army. And I really need a Motrin, or anything... ice would be fantastic."

"If the power's on at the airport, we'll find ice. Maybe that Motrin, too."

The Humvee fishtailed when Blum slammed on the brakes, but he kept it centered in the street. "Airport? They've overrun every airport in the country. What's our next choice?"

Archer shifted, trying to relieve the strain on his back and address Blum without grimacing. "Relax, it's actually a regional airfield. Just drive. I'll explain when we get there."

***

Blum crossed the Susquehanna and followed Continental Avenue to Danville Airport. "Well, calling it an airport seems a bit of a stretch." Blum was reacting to the small sign calling out the likewise-sized airfield nestled between vast fields of newly emerging corn. "I see a light! Lord, please, I'm begging you, let there be a fistful of Motrin and buckets of ice inside."

Archer slid from the Humvee and stood perfectly still. The spasm twisting his spine threatened to drop him if he so much as blinked.

"Looks like you could use some ice, too."

Archer jolted and his knees buckled. "Jesus H! Let a guy know when you're creeping up on him."

"Really, you didn't hear me?" Archer risked a painful glance at Blum. The man stood less than two feet away and had a thick tree branch tucked under his armpit. "I'm a walking jackhammer."

"I'm not convinced I'll make it to the office."

"Well, as you can see, I can't help you." Blum wiggled the branch under his left arm. "So, suck it up. We've gotta get inside. Lollygagging outside isn't an option."

\*\*\*

Blum tensed, then relaxed when the cold-pack met his swollen ankle. "Oh, yeah that's the stuff!"

Archer's head lulled toward Blum, then lifted slightly off the army surplus cot. Blum had just spoken, of that he was sure, but the man now sat with his eyes closed and slack-jawed in a leather office chair next to the airfield's communication hub.

"So, how the hell did you end up here?"

"Thought you were lights-out," Archer answered, oddly relieved Blum was still awake. "PA is slowly going dark... hospital had a little over three-hundred patients. CENTCOM patched our unit together to evac them to the one-six-seven airlift wing for transport to the interior. We were, uh, about two-thirds through..." Archer trailed off, his thoughts drifting to the slaughter happening a dozen miles away.

"You did what you could," Blum said, trying to ease the guilt clouding Archer's features. "How'd they find you?"

"This place," he answered, waving his hand around the airfield's office. "Private jets started arriving from the east coast a couple days after we secured the hospital. Low on fuel and carrying plenty of infected elite. The pricks spilled into the city like locusts. We just didn't have enough boots."

Blum shook two more expired aspirin from the bottle, dry swallowed them, and tossed the rest to Archer. "How's the back?" he asked, changing the subject. He knew how the story ended.

"Ice helps, aspirin's better. How long till they show up at our doorstep?"

"That depends. How many people were still in the hospital?"

"Hundred and four, counting what's left of the security force."

Blum sat forward, pain and exhaustion battling for control of his body. "We've got an hour. They can smell us. Once they latch onto our sent, they'll be like bloodhounds flushing rabbits."

Archer rose to his elbows and stared at Blum. "I was in Central Park when New York City fell," Blum began, responding to Archer's doubtful gaze. "The horde that showed up late to the party *here* slaughtered my squad and thousands of civilians *there*. They don't rest, they march and eat. That's it. I escaped them in a small town called Haven a little over thirty-six hours ago and they're already here. We've got an hour."

Archer swung his legs over the cot's edge and struggled to a seated position, then nodded at the radio. "Should we call for evac?"

Blum eased back in the chair. "Radio's been on the entire time we've been here. It's... quiet."

Archer nodded. They were on their own.

# Chapter 11

"We're going to die."

Belinda Harding shushed Patrick and brushed matted strands of hair from his damp face. "Quiet, Patrick. Our soldiers are out there fighting right now. You'll see, we'll be fine," she whispered. "You just have to stay quiet."

"They can smell my blood; they know I'm in here. Get me the hell out of this room!"

Nurse Harding mashed the plunger, pushing 20 milligrams of morphine into the panicking man's IV bag, his thrashing body stilled a moment later.

Belinda rested her hand on the pistol she'd taken from a soldier's ruined body and stared at the room's blockaded door. The hospital had grown quiet. What she'd told Patrick was merely a comforting lie, one she had desperately wanted to believe.

A startled yelp eked from her throat as a metal tray slid from the heap and clanged to the floor.

Was it the pitch-colored eyes, sinewy frame, or the ease with which it pushed through the wreckage she'd piled in front of the door? It didn't matter. Her body had seized, freezing her hand on the cool blue steel in her lap.

The infected tilted its head, shedding small bits of debris she thought resembled flesh, from its long beard, then focused on her hand. Her body twitched, willing itself to move, to shoot the monster casually strolling toward her. Stuttering sobs tugged at her bottom lip — its stench swallowed her, yet her hand remained paralyzed. "Please don't let this happen."

The infected met her whispered plea with rasping laughter as it fell on Patrick's unmoving body. Black eyes locked on hers as its head jerked back and forth before liberating a jagged slab of the unconscious man's neck.

Her body lurched forward in a feeble attempt to escape and sent the gun tumbling from her lap and skittering across the floor. She rocked forward again and nearly struggled to her feet when the gurney holding Patrick's mutilated body suddenly appeared in front of her.

Her mouth twisted in a soundless scream as realization found her. This monster was going to force her to watch his ghastly feast.

# Chapter 12

"Abel for Helpful Stranger person. Come in Stranger person, over."

Finn glared at his helmet, or, more precisely, its attached radio headset. This was Abe's fourth call.

"He's not going to stop, is he?" Aislin whined from the kitchen.

"He's not human, or normal, or stable."

"Abel for Helpful Stranger person. Come in Stranger person, over."

"I should've never taught him how to use the radio," Finn mumbled, as he watched Nic's guard team pass in front of his picture window. "That's my girl," he whispered when she didn't look or even side-eye in his direction. "On duty and focused."

She had to be dog-tired from Strike Team Training, but until they replaced her on the guard team, she'd be pulling twelve hour days. Yet, the set to her jaw told him she was present and determined to keep her home safe. "So damn sexy."

"Abel for Helpful Stranger person. Come in Stranger person, over."

"That's it! I'm going back to work. Digging trenches is more enjoyable than listening to that lunatic. I'm telling you now, if any infected show up today, I'm bringing them inside the fence and feeding your friend to them!"

"You going to Randy and Kit's after work?"

"I wasn't. Lynn was supposed to spend the night here. But if Abe's coming over — I'll go to her place."

"Abel for Helpful Stranger person. Come in Stranger person, over."

Finn glanced at the radio, then back to Aislin. "How's she doing?"

"She's angry... like the rest of us. She's been watching Randy's old Bruce Lee movies and teaching herself how to fight. It's a good outlet for her anger."

"You helping her with learning how to fight?"

"I will, in time. But for now, I want to watch her character develop. If she gets frustrated and quits, I'll teach her how to shoot. If she gets frustrated and keeps swinging, I'll teach her how to fight *and* shoot."

"Abel for Helpful Stranger person. Come in Stranger person, over."

"Oh my God, answer him!" Aislin barked as she stormed toward the radio.

"How's the trench coming? I missed Ann's update yesterday."

"How can you ignore that, that... he sounds like a robot!"

"The trench?"

"We've got about two-hundred yards left. We'd be done by now, but we've been getting harassed more every day. They're showing up in ones and twos, no hordes — yet. Guards put 'em down quick enough, but it still brings our work to a halt."

"Are you wearing the welding sleeves I found?"

Aislin clamped down on her flaring anger when she saw the raw worry creasing his features. This wasn't him scaring off her date. "I am. And I have your Sig with one in the chamber."

"That's my girl." He smiled, but worry still clouded his eyes.

"Abel for Helpful Stranger person. Come in Stranger person, over."

"I'm leaving! I'll throat punch him if I see him!"

\*\*\*

"You're sure you were talking into the microphone?"

"*Yes*, Helpful, I was talking into the mic. They were powered up and connected correctly!"

"Huh, that's odd. I didn't hear anything. And you say you called out three times?"

"Nine times... nine!"

"Well, they worked during training, not sure what happened. I'll get you a fresh set tomorrow."

Abe glared at Finn, then picked his helmet up and talked into the mic. "I hate you!" he said as he heard his own voice rattle through Finn's headset in the living room. "Now, tell me what's going on. Why all the hardcore GI training?"

Finn leaned forward and slid a folded piece of paper across the table, but his amused grin never faltered.

Abe startled, and started tapping a finger on the pictures, his head shifting between the paper and Finn.

"What? You're creeping me out, Abe. Are you having a stroke? Blink once if you're having a stroke."

"That's Sampson, and the Asian fella. Why do you have their pictures?"

Finn's brow furrowed as his mischievous grin faded. "How'd you know his name?"

The Sergeant's reddening face stopped Abe mid-way through his explanation. "What'd I say? You look pissed — really pissed."

Finn pushed away from the table and stood. "They had them — knew exactly where they were, could have ended this mess weeks ago. Why didn't we do anything? We just watched as they chewed New York to pulp."

"Are you asking me?" Abe said meekly while glancing around the quiet house. "What the hell was I supposed to do?"

"No — CENTCOM! They were *monitoring* the situation attempting to verify the report's authenticity. Now they want us to hunt these pricks down."

"Whoa! Timeout... hunt them? Where? I'm not going to New York!"

"Abe, radio the team. We need to talk."

## Chapter 13

O'Brien crouched behind an HVAC unit as the Humvee closed to within fifteen hundred feet, then raised his eyes over the edge. They hadn't seen another human, military or otherwise, in over a week.

He watched its approach while his internal debate raged. They didn't need help. They had plenty of food, still had power, and enough fuel to run the hotel's generator for weeks once the grid failed. He glanced at his AR — they also had enough weapons and ammunition.

"This is O'Brien," he whispered into his walkie. "We've got a military Humvee northbound on eighteen — stay low — let them pass."

"Why? They might have info, and we need more ammo."

"Damn it, Billy, we've got plenty of ammo and the government is still broadcasting updates. We don't need any trouble. Let them pass!"

From over his shoulder, O'Brien checked the rooftop guard stations and nodded. His men had taken cover.

*** 

"We going to make contact?" Archer asked while scrutinizing the hotel's roofline.

"Nope. If they wanted a visit, they wouldn't have taken cover. I've crossed paths with a couple *communities*. None of them were interested in helping. Most made that clear by pointing large caliber hunting rifles at my forehead. And that hotel has, what, one, possibly two hundred rooms with, presumably, equal numbers of armed residents. We're about a hundred miles from our target. I'm not tempting fate. We're too close."

"About that target?"

"I'd tell you, but I'd have to kill you," Blum chuckled. "Look, I'll understand if you ask me to spin into that place — see if they'll let you stay. But I'm not telling you where we're going. What if you go rogue, gather up a bunch of military wannabe whack-jobs, and storm the place? I'd be forced to kill you. You'd be mad. It would turn into a whole thing. Life's complicated enough."

"I'm good. But this target better have soft beds and a gourmet kitchen."

"Brother, you have no idea!"

\*\*\*

Denny O'Brien waited for Billy in the lobby. The '70s era hotel, in Sharon, PA, was once the embodiment of the self-contained family resort craze. Now, by any standard, it was garish and dated. Its lobby, steps away from an indoor swimming pool, which anchored its artificial, indoor courtyard, surrounded by dozens of rooms and their balconies, reeked of chlorine and stagnant water.

He glanced to the balconies where freshly laundered clothes hung limp from lines strung from one balcony to the next and supplies gained through barter sat piled against sliding glass doors. He strained to hear the sound which made all of this worth it — the delightful screeching of children playing in the distance, blissfully unaware of the horrors awaiting them beyond the walls of the refuge he'd built.

But, as always, the hollow eyes of their parents muted the joyful sound. These refugees were painfully aware of the chaos outside this sanctuary and torn between the relief of being alive and enduring the hellish imprisonment of merely surviving. His reminder of the lives depending on his leadership, his every decision, came from those slowly fading eyes.

"Let's talk, Billy."

The young hardhead responded by stalking toward O'Brien, his anger bubbling under stony features. "Make it quick. I have to relieve Marla on baby duty."

"Walk with me," O'Brien said as he slipped his arm around Billy's shoulders. "Never do that again," he whispered harshly when they cleared the lobby. "If you disagree with one of my decisions, approach me one on one. We need to show a unified front or this whole thing falls apart."

"I'll do it wherever and whenever I see you making a bad call. That was a bad call!" Billy growled while shrugging O'Brien's arm off.

"Could you see inside that Humvee? How many people were inside? Did they make radio contact? Were they military or a bunch of civilians who hijacked a military vehicle?"

"We'll never know, will we? We've practiced for outside contact extensively — have protocols in place! They could've helped us with supplies!"

O'Brien grabbed Billy's arm and spun him — forcing them face to face. He may be ten years Billy's senior, but he'd have no problem knocking him on his ass. "Or, they could have jumped out, guns blazing. Is Marla ready to be a single mother? Every life in this building is our responsibility, *my* responsibility. I talked all of you into moving here, told you I could be trusted, that I'd keep you safe. Inviting unknowns into our home goes against that pledge."

Billy's glare never softened, but he knew better than to test O'Brien's right hook. "Such a fearless leader, the great Denny O'Brien, still on patrol, still guarding his community. News flash, you're not a cop anymore. You're a refugee, just like the rest of us."

O'Brien leaned forward, halving the distance to Billy. "And you're just an ex-convict I took pity on. Don't press your luck."

## Chapter 14

"Go, go, go!" Finn shouted, sending Strike Team Alpha scrambling toward their target for the ninth time. "It's a new day, yesterday's gone, tomorrow isn't promised. But if it arrives, we'll be ready to beat it down!" They'd proven his assumption wrong. The news he'd held back hadn't negatively affected their training. Although he was correct in one respect, it had changed their approach. They'd become laser-focused... most of them had, anyway.

"News flash... it's empty. It's always empty," Abe yelled as they neared the front door.

"You'll thank me when we stumble into one that isn't empty!" Finn wheezed under the strain of his full kit.

"You can always quit, Abe," Stone roared between choked breaths. "If you're not going to quit, zip it. Your whining makes my head hurt."

"Listen to you two huffing and wheezing like a couple of old men sliding their walkers too fast! Maybe we should add calisthenics, whip you boys into shape."

Although his face glistened with sweat, Abe was holding up remarkably well; a development that wasn't sitting well with Finn. "Shut up and breach the door, Abe!"

"You know something, Helpful. This is the part I hate most. I'm really not breaching anything. The door's unlocked. I just reach out, turn the knob, and walk in."

"For the millionth time, take it up with Ann. If you talk her into letting us destroy the door, we'll do it. When I asked, she said, *sure, as long as you and your sister plan to live there.*"

"Outta the way," Stone yelled as he shoved Abe from the breach position. "I want to go home. The longer your jaws flap, the longer it'll be until that happens."

"I got it, Stone. Get back in formation. We breach on three!"

A solid thirty years had passed, maybe longer, since the brothers had invented a reason to scrap, but Stone's hard shove ended the drought. Abe tumbled backwards, landing hard and square on his kit. Air rushed from his lungs, but he still had enough to start throwing punches.

"Should we break them up?" Gage asked as he shuffled away from the wrestling Willings boys.

"Give 'em a minute to work it out." Finn's head tilted. They were fighting like... brothers, very young brothers brawling over a favorite Hot Wheel or the last Cherry Pop Tart. Feeble slaps and occasional halfhearted punches landed between WWE style wrestling moves. He knew how it would end.

"My eye! You poked me in my eye!" Abe screeched.

"There it is," Finn chuckled. "Alright, now that you little guys got that out of your systems, we'll wrap it up."

"I'm disappointed in you, Helpful," Abe grunted as he helped Stone to his feet and squinted through his left eye. "What if we got injured? You're down two vital team members. But you didn't even try to break us up."

"Well, Abe, as a trained soldier, I assessed the situation and determined the slap fest you and Stone were engaged in was more comical than dangerous. And ..."

"Sergeant!" Billings interrupted as he ran down the street holding his radio. "It's FOB Olmsted — Captain Hall."

"Tell him we need those supplies!" Abe shouted as Finn stepped away from their huddle.

\*\*\*

"Get out!" Randy blurted.

"I won't. Stanley and his caravan refused to enter the refugee center."

"Why should we care? He'll be dead soon, if not already, not a chance he makes it on his own."

"Because, Abe, he's a man with a reason to hate us. They wanted to give us a heads up in case he decides to come for his proverbial pound of flesh."

"Ain't this some shit? I knew we'd eventually have to tangle with living enemies — but Stanley wasn't what I had in mind. I think we'll be fine. Any word on those supplies?"

"Regardless, we'll add extra foot patrols. An enemy who knows the layout, defenses, and force size he's attacking... that's a dangerous enemy."

"Um, Helpful, I asked a question."

"I know."

Abe waited for Finn to continue — he didn't. "Well? Are we getting more supplies?"

"The req form is making its way up the chain. We'll know in a few days."

"Couple things. During our meeting last night, you said the military was pushing for civilian partnerships, to include *supplies*. Did you remind them that, as a tax-paying citizen, I already approved their purchase of said equipment? Now, I simply want what's rightfully mine."

"We and ours," Randy chimed.

"Somehow," Finn said with a smirk, "I don't think they care."

Abe's head snapped toward the echoing gunfire. "Where's your daughter, niece... Abigail?"

"Aislin."

"Whatever. Where is she?"

"Working the trench," Finn yelled as he ran to catch up to Abe, who bolted for the fence the instant shots were fired.

Nic pulled even with Finn and slammed a magazine with live ammo into her rifle. "Drop your empty mags — go hot!" she yelled, the clatter of hollow plastic bouncing off pavement soon followed. "She's going to be fine." Nic tried to sound confident.

As if responding to her words, the gunfire increased. "All teams to the west trench line," Finn yelled into his mic. His command was moot. Donovan's team was already at the main gate. He was sure others were also en route. "Nic, she's the only family I have."

## Chapter 15

The pressure in his chest had risen in tandem with the thickening air outside. Billy's undermining posture, in the days since they'd let the Humvee pass, had increased the hotel's already oppressive atmosphere tenfold. And now, cracks were forcing the refugees into opposing camps. The community he'd built would soon shatter.

O'Brien drained his last Iron City, surveyed his single room, and set the empty can on the nightstand, careful to line it up perfectly with the condensate left behind when it was cold. He glanced at the mini-fridge — it still held a few Yuengling Lagers — but he'd reached his daily allotment.

"My rules suck!" he grumbled and snatched the empty can from the stand and reared back. "O'Brien has the rock with three seconds on the shot clock — it's a fade away jumper for the win!"

The can clanked off the trash bin's lip and floated inches above its opening — he didn't see if he sank the three-pointer. The alarm blaring through the hotel made it unimportant.

"Someone talk to me. What's happening?" he yelled into his walkie as he ran into the hallway.

"Perimeter alarm triggered, south side."

"Sammy, do you have eyes on what triggered it?"

"Negative, the trees are blocking my... hold, I have movement. Shit, shit, shit! Send every gun we have to the roof."

"How many?"

"Hundreds."

\*\*\*

O'Brien skidded to a stop next to Sammy. His mouth fell open, then slammed shut. Their numbers were staggering.

His features strained. What were they doing? They stood motionless, staring at the hotel. Why?

A ripple at the rear of the herd rolled forward as a figure pressed ahead, pushing and shoving its way through the pack. "Sammy, I need your binoculars."

O'Brien adjusted the focus while he searched for the figure cutting through the crowd. The monster stood behind the waste-high cyclone fence, gripping it as if preparing to vault over. Then leaned forward and looked directly into O'Brien's eyes.

"It's... *thinking*! Sammy," he said, pivoting to face his friend, "kill them. Everyone, open fire!"

O'Brien dropped his scope's crosshairs on the location the *thinking* monster had been. It was gone — lost in the surge of infected pouring over the fence.

At his core, he knew it was wrong. The thing should have been there. Instinct told him it was leading the assault, but from where he didn't know, nor did he have time to find it, because hundreds of its brethren were flowing toward his home.

The infected fell in waves as the withering fire pummeled their ranks. His community had a chance. O'Brien's hope faded as dozens more burst from the tree line, trampling the infected cut down by the maelstrom raining on them from above. *They held back. These are reinforcements.*

He released his rifle's foregrip and flexed his hand, warding off the cramp building in his forearm, then risked a glance around the rooftop. Armed men and women stood shoulder to shoulder, hell-bent on living. Bolstered by the fierceness burning in their eyes, O'Brien rejoined the fight.

Had an hour passed, or merely ten minutes? He didn't know, as the gunfire slowed, then ceased. But not a soul moved. Each kept their weapon trained on the killing field, each waiting for a third wave to rush from the trees.

The stillness broke when O'Brien found Billy's eyes. He returned the man's stiff nod — the first step in mending their damaged relationship.

"Billy, Sammy, let's round up half a dozen strong backs. We need to clear the grounds A-SAP or we'll be knee deep in rats by morning."

Ignoring the thick blue smoke stinging their eyes, the trio waded through the damp evening air, tapping the shoulders of the men who'd clear their home of the dead as the rest of their force inched to the roof's edge, surveying the carnage below.

"Alright," he started as he pulled the rooftop access door open, "we start at the west corner..."

O'Brien's eyes went wide; his mouth moved but only wet gurgling escaped. Pain found him an instant later, followed by understanding. Done feasting on the bodies inside the hotel, the infected spilled from the door in a blur.

His body jerked violently, then folded to the roof. He tried to stand, but his legs refused. Unable to move, he watched the infected with the intelligent eyes chew frantically, then snap its head back and swallow.

The monster's black eyes seemed to smile as it kneeled next to him. He wanted to bat its beard from his face, but could only lie there, enduring its tickle as the infected sniffed the air around his prone body. A sputtering cough racked his chest as he gasped for air, but pulled blood deep into his lungs.

As he strained to hear the joyous sound of children laughing, he realized that the world had ended. Humanity couldn't withstand a creature willing to sacrifice hundreds, send them to be churned to mash, to allow only a handful to survive.

He closed his eyes tight, again searching for the laughter, but heard only the screams of his community being slaughtered.

A tear traced his jaw, then fell away — they had trusted him, he promised them they could.

***

Sampson's vision cleared as he swiped gore from his eyes. The hunger had returned, it never rested, and their food was always scarce.

Crouched at the roof's edge, a faded scent reached him through death's stench. It was faint — old, but distinct and familiar. One he'd been following — the fighter had been close. *He's searching for other fighters, and those fighters are protecting food. We will find you.*

Sampson rose to his full height and spun to find his waiting legions. He grimaced — he hadn't sensed them approach.

They were fewer now, and they were hungry.

# Chapter 16

Abe rounded the corner and shrugged off his kit while zigzagging through the chewed earth hoping to avoid enemy crosshairs. The backhoe was two hundred yards away, and he pressed forward, straining his legs to carry his weight faster than they ever had.

Dust and smoke billowed around the trench crew's location, but he was able to take a quick tally. The team should have stood ten strong. Why was he counting twenty?

His question was answered at one hundred yards — infected had attacked, not humans, and they were rampaging among the crew.

"Hold fire," he huffed over the radio. "We've got friendlies in our sightlines. I count ten infected — minimum. We'll be hand-to-hand."

Abe slid his blade free and focused on the cluster to his right. "Finn, take the center with Nic and Gage. Randy, Stone, you're with me. Strike Team Bravo, flank the backhoe, trench side."

*How'd he know?* "Abe, only one of us gives orders... *this* time it's you."

"No shit, Helpful. After we handle these infected, rally at the backhoe's blindside. That's where the gunfire's coming from. We'll catch them in an 'L' crossfire."

Abe didn't check to see if Randy and Stone followed, nor did he wait for confirmation they'd even heard his orders. The infected had surrounded someone and that person couldn't wait.

Steps from the cluster, an infected twisted from the horde and crumpled to the hard pack. Abe seized the opportunity, went to a knee, and slammed his blade through the monster's crown.

Stars burst through his vision, his body jolted right, and spun to the ground. Abe scrambled to right himself, but was pinned facedown. Coughs rattled his body as dust from the ravaged land was pulled into his lungs. His vision blurred. He couldn't find Stone or Randy.

A raspy growl at his ear pushed cold air, reeking of rancid meat, onto his cheek. "Oh, bullshit!" Abe rocked his body fiercely left. The infected slid from his back, but didn't restart its attack. Except for its gnashing maw, it laid perfectly still.

"Man, that's nasty," Abe mumbled when he noticed the unhealthy angle of its neck. He pushed his blade through the pitiful creature's temple, then spun to join the fight.

"'Bout time you boys showed up!"

"Abe, I'm fully engaged!" Randy grunted as he forced a zombie's shredded face onto his K-Bar.

"Did you see the monster attacking me and not care, or were you hoping I'd get murdered?"

"You talking about the thing with the noodle neck? Really? If you can't handle that bag of meat, take off your heels before you twist an ankle."

"Wasn't talking to you, Stone," Abe yelled as he yanked an infected to the ground and stomped on its neck. The monsters were so focused on the food at the center of their scrum, they hadn't noticed the trio attacking their rear flank.

Through a gap in their phalanx, Abe glimpsed a flash of red hair. "It's Arleen!"

"Abe, you said ten! There's more than ten!" Randy shouted. "And who the hell is Arleen?" He pivoted as Abe lowered his head, squared his shoulders, and rushed the monsters. Randy flinched when his friend's battle cry burst through his headset.

Abe's head led his body, his balance followed, and left his feet far behind. Air rushed from his lungs when he spurted through the infected and landed hard on his stomach. He'd met much less resistance than expected.

"You here to nap or fight?"

Arleen pivoted right, unleashed a roundhouse kick, which broke her target's neck, then sprinted in the opposite direction, leaped into the air and landed an equally devastating front kick. Her constant back-and-forth defense kept the infected at bay, but their noose was tightening — she was running out of time.

"Abel!" she hollered as she swept the legs of a charging infected.

Startled by a thud behind her, Arleen spun to find an infected crumpled at her feet. "Apparently, I'm here to make sure you don't get killed!"

Her elbow, sheathed in leather, raced toward his face and buckled Abe at his waist, but it still scraped roughly over his scalp before it slammed into a rotting jaw.

"You're not good at your job!"

The monster slithered to the ground and crashed against Abe's calves, forcing him into the void where Arleen had been an instant before. Unfolding from his crouch, he faded left to intercept a tracking zombie when it fell from sight.

The horde tumbled as Stone and Randy pummeled their ranks. "Let's move. That means you too, Arleen," Abe yelled as the last of the infected twisted to the hard pack.

"Abe, her name's Aislin," Randy huffed as they raced shoulder to shoulder toward the gunfire.

"Whatever! When we reach the backhoe, you break right with Alice. Link up with Bravo. Stone, you're with me... combat distance!"

They reached the backhoe and stopped. No one broke right, nor did they fall into combat distance. Instead, they stared at the field of death stretching from the giant yellow machine to the tree line, twenty yards away, where another wave was emerging.

"So many more than ten," Randy mumbled.

Abe took in the sections of completed trench and barrier. They displayed no signs of being breached. *They knew where to attack!*

"I hope you brought ammo." The voice was clear, too clear. The shooting had stopped, and the infected were shambling toward their position.

Abe spun. It was Jimmy, and he'd taken refuge atop the backhoe with most of his crew. "We lost Phil. Not sure where Aislin and Rick are, but we didn't see them fall. They hit fast, Abe. So damn fast."

Abe heard the strain of guilt in Jimmy's tone. This was his crew, his responsibility. He'd lost one and was imagining the others were also dead.

"Jimmy, I'm good," Aislin said from tiptoes over Randy's broad shoulders. Jimmy's head tilted skyward, thanking the Man he'd asked for just such an outcome.

"Abe for Finn, we're searching for someone named Rick."

"That package is secured. We're en route."

They flinched collectively when gunfire erupted from the trench. Donovan's team had taken up the fight.

"Hold fire," Abe ordered. "I have a plan."

\*\*\*

"You sure about this, Abe?"

"My plan means my balls on the line."

"Okay, but..."

"Randy, remember the final fight scene in *Zombieland*? The whirly ride thingy? Machines versus flesh... machines win!"

"Yeah, but you're not Columbus, and this isn't a movie. You're Abe, from Cleveland, who'll die for real."

"I'm good. Donovan's team has me covered if anything goes sideways. It'll save us a ton of ammo. Get everyone back inside the fence — now. They're closing."

Abe fired the John Deer 200D and it rattled to life belching black smoke. He concentrated on the controls. Jimmy's rushed instructions were foggy now that it was rumbling through his body. He mashed the pedal and released it when the behemoth lurched forward.

"Abe, you planning on doing something? Cuz now would be good," Donovan's voice in his headset broke his concentration and pulled his focus to the boom.

"Ha! Not today," he yelled as he yanked the boom's joystick hard right, spinning it, and the cab, in the same direction. Abe froze, he was like a kid on his first rollercoaster, and he couldn't release the stick.

Infected flashed through his vision as the boom leveled them with each pass. "Finn, safe to say these are Omega variants. Also, I'm getting a little sick," Abe radioed.

"Explain?" Finn replied, his voice muffled by the backhoe's thunderous power plant.

"They just keep coming. They see what's happening and what's causing it, but just keep charging. As for the sick part..."

"Let the joystick go."

"Are they dead? My eyes are closed."

"All dead."

***

Abe looked on as Jimmy's team pushed the dead into a pit they'd dug on the opposite side of the main road. "We needed a burn pit, anyway. But hoochie mama, that stinks."

Strike Team Alpha stayed on site as Jimmy's team worked and Strike Team Bravo cleaned up the stragglers lurking in the woods. Their gunfire had dropped off, becoming widely spaced and further away.

"Abel! Let's talk — now!"

"Sounds like dad's mad at you," Randy chuckled.

"Meh, he doesn't scare me."

"See, Abe, that's why people believe you're damaged, because Finn should scare you. He's trained to kill both quickly and efficiently," Stone said, as he scraped goo from his boot treads.

"Nah, he won't kill me. Plus, I've already proven I can outrun him. I'll be good."

"But his sister is faster than both of you. She'd be on you like stink on shit before you took your second step."

"Ah yes, my loyal brother, that's when you and my dearest friend would intervene. Together, we become an unbeatable trio of masculinity."

"Unbeatable trio of... *what*?"

"*Abel*! Front and center! NOW."

\*\*\*

"Never again. Have I made myself clear?"

"But..."

"Zip it! This team has one, I repeat, one leader. And, Abel, who would that be?"

"But Alice couldn't wait..."

"Answer my question!"

"Sure, it's you. But the next time Alice is in a jam, and you're lollygagging around, I'll let her know we have to wait for you to show up."

"For the last damn time, her name is Aislin. And she can take care of herself. She would've started shooting, but your enormous block head showed up. She didn't want to shoot you, so she stayed hand-to-hand. I told her, next time, take the shot!" Spittle sprayed from Finn's mouth, speckling Abe's scrunched features.

Abe dragged a hand down his face, then pretended to flick Finn's spit from it. "It usually takes people longer before they threaten to kill me. You're soft. Nor does your threat solve our problem."

Finn paced in front of Abe, glaring at him. His nostrils flared and jaw flexed.

"You don't see it, do you? You're mad — or getting madder — because you don't see our problem."

"I see a lot of problems. One of them is standing in front of me. So, tell me, what problem has your unbalanced brain identified?"

Abe wiped fresh spittle from his forehead. "Lower your hackles, Helpful. You're frothing."

Finn hard-stepped toward Abe, his nose brushing against his nemesis's. "You've reached the end of my patience."

"Okay, okay, relax. We need a better barrier. They keep showing up in these numbers, and they'll overwhelm the trench and push through our fence like it's papier mâché. That happens, not even your sister, as tough as she is, will be able to save us."

"Daughter," Finn corrected, his combative stance relaxing. "She can definitely fight."

Abe stifled his grin, *works every time*. "It's clear you had a part in her training. She's tough, an excellent addition to the community."

Finn's head sagged between slumped shoulders. "You're a crafty bastard."

"Nah, just an exceptional salesman."

Finn raised his head. He couldn't let what happened slide. "You can't do that. Confusion on the battlefield gets people killed. If you can't control yourself..."

"Got it. I need to behave. About that barrier."

Finn pinched the bridge of his nose. "It's getting dark, go home, Abe. We'll talk later."

"I'll go after we wrap up," Abe said, and turned to find the area empty. "Huh, suppose I'll see you at training tomorrow." He trudged toward the gate, smoldering that his friends had left him behind.

"Finn is stupid, Randy is stupid, the apocalypse is stupid... everything is stupid," Abe grumbled as he stomped up his driveway. A flash of movement in the picture window drew his attention to her face... her evil, smiling face. "Ah, the queen of stupid awaits."

## Chapter 17

"Stanley, I'm not comfortable with this. Please stop."

Crystal's head tilted. He kept tending to his subjects, as he'd taken to calling them, seemingly oblivious to her presence. He'd changed since their group secured the dog kennel, only minutes from their former home, and just days ago. Their second night, he began sneaking out with his trusty animal control pole, ensnaring infected, and housing the monsters in the property's outbuilding, where the dogs had once been kept.

The grounds, a beautiful plot of land atop a rolling knoll and skirted by mature oaks, had served the area's wealthy, providing a luxurious stay for their pampered pets.

He'd promptly released the few emaciated animals they'd found and began feeding the remains of others to his subjects. He'd become a ghoulish shell of the man she'd married.

The others were forbidden to enter Stanley's macabre sanctuary. He told them it was due to threat of infectious diseases lurking amongst the animal feces and festering carcasses, "a terrible place full of death and illness," he'd warned.

The property's primary structure, a stunning Victorian home, was large enough for the entire group to share comfortably, and sat adjacent to a wrought-iron gate and border fence of the same style.

Why he'd chosen this place or even knew it existed, Crystal could only guess.

"My dear worrywart," he hummed in his expected dismissive tone, "their humanity remains locked within their tragic shells. We are morally bound to set them on the path to redemption."

"Redemption! This from an agnostic! Tell me, what redemption are you referring to? The type you attempted at our home? We need food, weapons, and fuel. You should be scavenging with the others, trying to secure our safety!"

"My work is more important. I don't expect one with your stunted intellect to grasp the immensity of what I'm striving to accomplish. But, for you, I'll use lay terms. I can end this scourge, bring these sad souls back from the abyss... cure them!"

Crystal, accustomed to his demeaning opinion of her intelligence, brushed the insult aside with a wave of her hand. "How will you explain this when our friends find your demented workshop? They'll leave, Stanley — we can't survive without them!"

"Some will stay, some will go. To the traitors, I say good riddance."

Crystal startled and stumbled backwards as one of the caged monsters to her right slammed against the cyclone fencing. "You can't fix them!" she shrieked, as she continued her retreat.

"I haven't quite puzzled this group out," Stanley said, while indicating the cage holding the now thrashing infected. "They're... different from the others. More aggressive. I've had to separate them to ensure that once I cure them, they'll have bodies capable of being redeemed."

"Please, I'm begging you to stop."

"You're free to leave, to join the traitors in the wilds."

"I may do that!" Her chin jutted in defiance.

"I say good riddance," he mumbled, turning back to his subjects and sliding a wedge of rancid meat through the feed opening. "Good luck surviving without me. You've been a dependent leech since the day we met. I endure scarcely a shred of apprehension in parting ways with you."

Crystal flinched. She'd been a good wife, indulging his bizarre hobbies, defending him when their friends whispered awful things behind his back, feigning interest as he droned on about his meaningless days. To hear his true feelings — the sharpness of his tongue cut her deeply.

Crystal failed to respond to his rebuke in what he determined an acceptable amount of time. He turned and found she'd left. "I should have known you'd flee. Hopefully, you'll secure alternative accommodations."

The infected slammed against the cage again, and spat rancid meat to the floor. Stanley grinned. "Or maybe you'd serve humanity better if you remained."

# Chapter 18

"No more interwebs!"

Lu stopped at the front door. He'd spoken — for the first time in two plus weeks. "Happened a few days ago. Cell service is also down."

"This is bullshit! I wanted to see if people were still uploading videos — see how the rest of the country's faring."

Lu walked to the bottom of the staircase, and glanced apprehensively at the upstairs landing. This next move was tricky. If she asked if her silent treatment had ended, it may remind him, and restart the whole mess. If she didn't ask, he may accuse her of not caring and that she was assuming he'd worked through whatever perceived wrong was brought against him.

"I'm sorry about the bacon," she said and winced in anticipation of his response.

"I know, babe. Don't sweat the small stuff. You better get moving. Ann's waiting."

*Don't sweat the small stuff!* Lu bit the inside of her cheek, *I wasn't sweating, you were!*

Abe's sudden appearance on the landing startled her. "What? I didn't say anything, but if you want to go another round about your precious bacon..."

"Whoa, I said no sweat." *He has the nerve to sound incredulous.* "You should try to let things go. Holding onto anger isn't healthy, babe."

Abe's head snapped right, then left, his brow furrowed. "Did you hear that?"

Lu shook her head because, if she spoke, the verbal lashing she'd unleash would likely end their marriage.

Abe bounded down the stairs and froze. "There — again!"

"It's probably just Finn picking you up for training."

"Shush. Finn gave us the day off. It's two, possibly three, engines." He leaned forward, head slanted toward the door. "What *is* it?"

"Go check!" Lu yelled after sixty seconds of Abe standing still passed.

"It sounds like..." Abe's eyes widened and Lu thought his body vibrated. "They're here, holy shit! Finn came through!" He bolted for the door, slammed to a stop, spun, and hugged Lu. "They're here, babe." He was outside a flash later.

Lu watched him rush down the street, slap his helmet on, and throw excited punches at the sky.

"Randy, Stone, the supplies are here!"

"I'm at the gate with Stone. Three trucks, Abe. Three flipping trucks of supplies!"

As the gate came into view, he noticed the trucks idling outside the fence. "Why aren't they inside?" he asked as he joined Randy and Stone. "Shouldn't they be inside?"

"Something isn't right. Finn's been reviewing maps with the drivers and giving orders to his squad. The squad he *arrived* here with."

"I'm with Stone. Something's off," Randy agreed.

Abe's stomach went to butterflies when two of the trucks lurched toward them. They'd worried for nothing. "Oh yeah, here they come, boys. Finn was probably giving them directions on where to drop the containers when they..." Abe trailed off as the trucks accelerated past them, headed for the community's eastern perimeter, each holding one of Finn's men in their passenger seat.

The whine of a straining wench joined the hiss of hydraulics and pulled the trio's attention to the remaining truck. Why offload the container outside the fence on the trench's far side?

Abe flinched when the truck pulled forward and the container's front end slammed to the pavement. "We don't have the equipment to move a twenty-foot shipping container. What the hell is he thinking?" Abe was running for the gate's latch as he spoke. He had to stop this.

"Nah, ah, ah, only *real* military personnel outside the gate. Strict orders from Finn."

Abe's lips pulled into a tight line, his eyes screwed shut. Where'd she come from? "Nic, stop talking."

"Aw, you finally spoke to me, actual words. How sweet, but you aren't stepping foot outside the fence."

Abe faced the gate and laced his fingers through its links. His chest heaved rapidly as his head sagged.

"You okay? Looks like you're having a heart attack," Randy whispered.

Abe stiffened his back and shook his body. "Good, I'm good. We'll get the supplies, bring 'em in, and go on the offensive. I'm good."

Abe cringed as steel screeched against pavement — the truck was inching forward with the container in tow. Clangs and pings of interlocked metal grids springing from the container, forming large fabric-lined boxes, drowned out the revving diesel as the truck gained speed. Abe's jaw went slack when a massive front-end loader roared in and began filling the grids with dirt.

"What am I watching?" Abe uttered, barely above a whisper.

"It's like something from a Bugs Bunny cartoon."

"Actually, Randy, it's a HESCO RAID barrier."

"Nic, what's a HESCO RAID?"

"Well, Stone," Nic's voice raised an octave, ensuring Abe would hear, "RAID stands for Rapid In Theater Deployment Barrier. Finn secured them after the fiasco at the trench. Only took two days. Guess he can get supplies when *someone* isn't bugging him."

"Get supplies when some isn't bugging him," Abe mocked, his voice pitched and nasally.

"They'll have the entire community secured in a couple hours, including filling them. My man is dreamy."

"FINN, we need to talk!"

# Chapter 19

"What the hell?"

"Not the reaction I expected."

Abe turned to watch the truck rumbling in the distance. Its progress was astonishing. "Why didn't you get us one of these, I don't know, three weeks ago? I mean, my wife almost died getting the backhoe, we've spent weeks working on, on, this mess, and those monsters killed one of our trench crew."

Abe held Finn's gaze as he waited for an answer. "Well?"

"You done?"

Abe nodded, but never broke his hard stare.

"You, ah, recall the situation with the military abandoning my squad, correct? Don't answer, it's obvious you don't. So I'll make it simple for you. Before, Finn no get military stuff, now Finn do. Keep friends safe. Fight bad monsters. Took Abe's advice, built wall."

Abe's eyes narrowed. "Don't be a jackass, just say it... loud enough so everyone hears you."

*\*\*\**

"RAID Barrier, nice," Gage said as he joined Randy, Stone, and Nic a few feet from Abe and Finn's standoff. "Watching these things get installed always fascinated me. Simple and effective, I've seen them take direct fire from..." Gage trailed off, and followed their focus. "Oh shit, what's got his panties bunched this time?"

Randy shushed Gage with a finger to his own mouth. "It's getting good."

\*\*\*

Finn looked quizzically at Abe.

"Say it... tell everyone this barrier's been installed because I saw a problem you missed. How I care so deeply for them that I'm willing to sacrifice my mental wellbeing interacting with you. That I'm batting a thousand when it comes to securing our perimeter. Go on, say it."

\*\*\*

"I'll bet an MRE Finn punches him."

"I'll take that action, Stone," Randy said.

"Count me in. And double or nothing Abe says he can't keep fighting because Finn poked him in his eye."

"Sorry, Nic. That's a sucker's bet." Gage turned back to the faceoff as voices rose.

\*\*\*

"Say it! You know it's true, Helpful. Or are you worried you'll disappoint your *girlfriend* by admitting I'm smarter than you?"

"You don't see our problem, do you? You're overcompensating because you don't see it."

"Oh no — don't change the subject!" Abe's eyes shifted back and forth, everything looked as it had. "You're deflecting." Abe smiled smugly. "You're using my tactics. Not today, Helpful, I'm on to you!"

Abe ignored the engine growling behind him. He wouldn't give Finn the satisfaction by showing how impressed he was at the speed with which the barrier had been erected. He flinched when Finn's hand went up, waving the truck to their position. "Grandstanding is vulgar. The sign of a fragile ego."

\*\*\*

"Ohhh, so close. I thought that was it. He had Abe dead to rights."

"Ha, looks like you owe me an MRE, Stone."

"Randy, you've known Abe your entire life. Do you really think he's done jawing? You'll be forking over that MRE. We both know it."

\*\*\*

Abe flinched again when an airbrake released. This wasn't one of the trucks setting up the barrier, but an olive drab Kenworth, and it was inches from his side. He stepped back and scanned the vehicle, stopping at the trailer and its tarp which projected skyward with sharp angles. It hid something big, and Abe's eyes lit up. "Bradley?"

"Ha, you think I'd turn you loose in a Bradley?" Finn mocked as he ran to the cab, then hoisted himself to the driver's window.

\*\*\*

"Why the hangdog face?" Nic asked.

"I wanted a Bradley," Randy mumbled.

"What's a Bradley?"

"Go away, Nic. You're being hurtful."

\*\*\*

"It's a solution to the problem you didn't see," Finn said as he rejoined Abe. "Nic, guide him through the gate. His first stop is the southwest corner, ten feet off the fence. Gage, you're with Nic. The driver's going to need two spotters to navigate our streets."

"Supplies?"

"Nope. Rec form is still working its way through the chain of command. Those are MMGTs, and they're our force multiplier."

Abe shrugged, and shook his head.

"Mobile Multipurpose Guard Tower. Requested them with the barrier, FOB Olmsted reconfigured before they set up and were left with loads of unused perimeter security equipment. We claimed the leftovers. They said something about keeping you contained being a good idea and rushed them to us."

"I think I hate you."

"You don't." Finn chuckled as he walked away.

Abe spent a few minutes watching the barrier being assembled and smiled. It was exactly what they needed, and it was his idea. "Abel Willings, you're the man!"

\*\*\*

A trembling hand set binoculars on the bedside nightstand after the community erected the fourth tower. What were they? The urge to rush to them and beg for shelter was overwhelming. But patience was the better plan. How patient was the question.

A pat on the backpack resting on the floor answered the question of food; it was full of canned goods. The house, mercifully empty of both infected and their stench, would provide shelter indefinitely. The bed was lumpy, but better than the floor. The large knife would prove helpful if attacked, but aged hands would do little if the infected attacked in even small numbers.

"I'll observe them until I determine their *mood* for refugees."

# Chapter 20

Sampson noticed the lesions had grown worse during their foodless trek. They now covered many of his soldiers. Their cause was as mysterious as the white tendrils sprouting from some of the larger wounds. These were his earliest recruits — he needed them.

Sampson stopped. The flickering light ahead meant food was close. He led his soldiers from the road into the brush, which twisted its way across from the orange glow's edge.

His neck arched, lifting his nose into the night air, and froze. Charred wood laced with animal fat obscured all other scents. A memory flashed against his closed eyes... this food would be full and sluggish as they licked every morsel of their meal from greasy fingers. Easy quarry.

A thump spun Sampson. He crouched, coiled to strike. It was one of his soldiers, and it was on its back, thrashing in the brittle undergrowth. His soldier's body stiffened, a strangled rasp escaped its locked-open mouth.

A wild firethorn shrub pierced Sampson's flesh as he pushed his body from the ground and raced to quiet his soldier. His foot met little resistance as it crushed his soldier's neck, silencing it. Ignoring his downed soldier's snapping jaw, he spun toward the flickering glow.

\*\*\*

Blum heaved the last empty jerry can into the cargo rack. It had taken roughly two days to scavenge enough fuel to fill the Humvee's tank. They should, barring a lengthy detour, make it to their target with what he found.

The irony of where they'd run out of gas wasn't lost on him — mere feet from the state line. Fortunately, he'd managed to coast the Humvee into the below-grade median, which offered some cover. Nevertheless, they'd been dangerously exposed.

His ankle's muted protest had slowed his search, but it was healing. He couldn't say the same for Archer. The flyboy had only gotten worse in the days since they'd left Danville airport. Blum recognized it for what it was, at least one herniated disc.

"Smells good," Blum said as he approached the fire pit. They hadn't eaten since, he really couldn't remember, but it had been long enough that the smell filled his mouth with saliva.

"Never cooked wild rabbit. Hope it's edible." Archer stoked the fire as he spoke, avoiding eye contact with Blum. It was easy considering his bent posture angled his upper body downward.

"Hey, we'll find you a doctor. Until then, you're my wingman, so suck it up."

Archer's eyes remained downcast — he was a burden, not a wingman. He'd slowed their progress dramatically with his hourly need to stretch his back and chase away the pins and needles swarming over his right leg. He couldn't lift over five pounds or manage ten steps a minute. Hell, he wasn't even able to field dress the rabbits he and Blum were about to share.

"I'm in trouble, aren't I? My back is screwed and getting worse and we both know finding a competent doctor, let alone a surgeon, is unlikely."

"Yeah, but at least I can outrun you if we get chased."

Archer swung his head toward Blum, the man's features were flat, unreadable, until his lips quivered. "Rotten prick." Archer's chuckle built to laughter, then hysterical howling when Blum joined in.

\*\*\*

White tendrils split the immobilized soldier's chest cavity, then raced toward the weeping lesions covering the feeble soldier's body where they plunged into the wounds, knotted to the slowly growing wispy strands, and pulled them along to the next festering gash.

Sampson didn't notice the grotesque manifestation — the men playing with fire had distracted him.

A snarling grin creased his features. They'd found the fighter, and he wouldn't escape again. He turned to his soldiers. They were waiting for him to start the hunt.

\*\*\*

"You hear that?" Archer looked up, a half-eaten thigh bone suspended an inch from his mouth.

"Yep — get your ass in the Hummer." Blum stood and leveled his M4 in the direction of the snapping twig. The firelight danced against the heavy scrub brush, casting shadows, and giving movement to every surface it touched. *Perfect camouflage*!

The brush line was at most twenty yards away, with only the turnpike's littered pavement between them. He'd have 14 seconds to find cover if the infected were walking — but they wouldn't be walking.

"Why don't I hear you shuffling?"

Archer didn't answer, Blum spun, prepared to find they'd been flanked, and his wingman dead. "You're kidding, right?"

"They hate fire. I'm covering our six. It won't stop them, but it'll slow their advance." Archer grunted as he tossed a flaming branch into the night sky behind them. Sparks erupted into a fountain when it slammed to the ground. Several small fires flared seconds later.

"Get in the Hummer! We're in no condition for a rolling battle."

"One more," Archer grunted as he heaved the flaming branch to the right of the growing fires he'd already started. The branch flashed through the air, then exploded as it clanged against a metal pole and rattled the overhead sign it supported, raining embers into the brush.

His first step toward the Humvee hurt, the second buckled his knees, but he swallowed his scream. He couldn't pull Blum's attention from the brush line and give the infected an open path. Archer groaned as the scabbed wounds on his legs split open, but he didn't stop crawling. He had to make it on his own. Their lives depended on it.

*\*\*\**

Sampson rushed forward, then stopped to allow his soldiers to continue the charge. He pivoted to face them when they didn't move. The light flickering in their black eyes told him why.

*Then I eat alone*! He seized a soldier in a vicious headlock, spun back toward the food, and shoved the struggling beast forward.

\*\*\*

Blum's M4 tracked the rustling brush, but found no target. Was it really an infected or possibly a stray dog, deer, maybe some other animal drawn by the scent of charred rabbit and searching for an easy meal?

He cursed himself for leaving his night vision goggles in the Humvee's cargo hold. *Sure would be nice to see what's hunting us!* The mystery was solved when a lone infected burst through the brush and staggered to its knees.

It took Blum a second, maybe two, to acquire his target — it hadn't moved, or even tried to. It simply stared at him through his M4's optics.

Blum jerked as his rifle sent a three-round burst into the brush directly behind the kneeling monster, then shifted his aim left and right, before ending the kneeling infected with a single green tipped round.

"Roll ass, Gimpy, we're running out of time!"

\*\*\*

Fluff leaked from the graze wound on Sampson's arm as he stalked closer to the flames set loose by the weak fighter. He crouched and peered through a narrow gap in the foliage. The crawling man had become an irresistible opportunity.

Sampson glanced at the fighter who had almost ended his hunt, the man's eyes remained fixed on where he'd sacrificed his soldier. This would be an easy kill!

A crackling whoosh pushed sizzling embers into Sampson's vision. He batted them from the air, but they came in ever-increasing waves. Smoke clouded the air and mixed with the stench of burning flesh. For only the second time since the hunger had found him, Sampson experienced pain. A searing throb grew with intensity as the air thickened with shimmering ash.

The understanding was sudden and jolted him to his feet as he slapped at the smoldering rags covering his legs. He backed deeper into the brush, his steps slow and controlled before a sensation he hadn't experienced since long before the hunger gripped him and sent him rushing forward. Fear!

\*\*\*

Archer's hands flailed, but couldn't beat back the monster dragging him across the brittle median grass. It had latched onto his flight suit's collar and was pulling it, and him forward, shortening his reach as it garroted his windpipe.

"Stop struggling, Gimpy. It's me, and your little Fire Marshal Bill maneuver might have worked. It'll probably kill us, but it definitely slowed them down."

At the Humvee, Blum bent to help Archer to his feet when the brush line exploded. Infected, engulfed in flame, rushed toward them then crumpled to the ground, fueling the growing fire as they rolled across the rain-starved terrain.

"It can't be!" he mumbled. Another flash of a long beard, retreating into the overgrowth, removed his doubt; the infected from Central Park had found him again.

# Chapter 21

Sampson slithered from the large concrete culvert running under the turnpike and whipped his head back and forth, then swiped at the stubborn muck, blurring his vision. Wisps of smoke still floated from his bare and scorched chest. But the stagnant water had quelled the worst of the flames and left his body wounded but intact. Static blitzed his thoughts. Again, he shook his head. He needed to feed.

He searched the air for his soldiers, but found only acrid smoke carrying the stench of charred skin. The night air crackled and hissed as he trudged up the embankment, hidden in the thick overgrowth. This side of the road remained untouched by the raging fire, but its heat still reached him in scorching ripples.

Lumps of flesh, dozens of them, marked the place his army had fallen. Sampson was alone.

\*\*\*

"I'm telling you, they're camped in the median. They must have started the fire."

"How many?" Jacob asked, while he eyed Paul suspiciously.

"I already told you — two. And stop looking at me like that. I didn't set the damn fire. Those military boys must've done it. You'll see when we get there."

Paul Snyder's pace quickened. It was dark, and the zombies hunted at night, but the sooner he showed his asshole brother the campsite, the sooner his family would stop blaming him for setting the fire which had forced them to abandon their homestead and relocate closer to Oak Tree Lake.

He'd discovered the encampment at sun up, during his scavenging mission, and noted their location with plans of finishing his search, linking up with his brother, doubling back, and making contact with the soldiers. But the fire had sent him scrambling for safety.

He pushed aside a juniper branch and went to a knee. The soldiers were gone.

"All I see is a big ass brush fire."

Paul scanned the area through his rifle's scope. "Fire pit! In the median ten yards off the road, under the sign."

Paul glanced at Jacob when he didn't answer. "Do you see it?"

"It's not the fire pit I'm worried about. Check out the ground about ten yards southeast of the pit."

"What the hell! Looks like an ambush."

"If it was an ambush, your soldiers went literal scorched earth."

Jacob's head snapped toward his brother, pulled by his sharp gasp. The thickening smoke couldn't hide the terror in Paul's eyes.

"One of them is still alive. We've got to help."

Paul staggered when his brother yanked him back by his tactical vest, then pushed him to the ground. "That person is dead. You won't do a damn thing except get yourself killed."

"We can't just let them suffer!"

"We won't," Jacob mumbled while staring blankly at the lump of burning humanity struggling to escape the inferno. His rifle boomed a moment later. "It's over. Let's get back to camp."

Jacob tried to scream but couldn't, infected jaws had crushed his windpipe. He struggled to break free, but the beast held fast. His rifle clattered to the earth as he thrashed against the soot-covered infected, desperate to create enough space between them to pull his knife. His struggle ended when the monster drove him to the ground and splintered his spine on an exposed oak tree root.

As Jacob's consciousness faded, the monster shifted to untouched flesh and shoved Jacob's head to the side. It came to rest facing his brother. He tried to cry out, to warn Paul, tell him to run, but only spat blood to his chin.

Jacob's last sight was his dead brother's frozen scream.

# Chapter 22

Finn pushed air though puffed cheeks, offsetting the sting of Jameson's as he poured another shot, the last the bottle had to offer. He hadn't indulged in *Jamey* since the world went sideways... but it had to be longer than a month? After his call with Malloy and the full JCS, or what passed as the Joint Chiefs of Staff, he figured he'd earned a bender.

"Is this the only bottle?"

"Of Jamey — yes." Aislin kept her puffy eyes downcast when she joined Finn at the dining room table. She'd been crying since Finn started drinking, and didn't want him to see them.

"Welp, suppose I should get everyone together. Can't have them finding out from my squad. I have to control the message."

"Abel for Helpful Stranger, come back Helpful Stranger."

"Him? That's the guy you're leaving us with?"

Finn shot the Jameson and slammed the glass to the table. "He's fearless, just ask him. He'll tell you."

"Helpful Stranger, come in Help..."

"Abe, as always, your timing is impeccable."

"Do you know what I'm doing?" Abe huffed, his voice jostled.

"From the sounds of it, I don't think I want to know."

"Mind out of the gutter, Finn. I'm running — in the dead zone between the fence and the HESCO. Why am I able to run in the dead zone, Finn?"

Finn's lips twisted and his face scrunched. "I don't think I care. But I need to talk to the team."

"Of course you don't care because you have military grade weapons. The rest of us have to pray the barriers hold and the trench is deep enough, without our defensive obstacles — they won't. Which brings me to my next point."

"Still don't care. Stay where you are. We'll come to you."

\*\*\*

Abe recoiled as Nic grew nearer. "Man, what the hell happened to you? I mean, you're always a bit on the hagfish side, but holy smokes!"

Bracketed by Nic and Aislin, Finn looked Abe up and down. His running shorts struggled to cover his corded thighs and the man's shoulders and arms bulged around his tank top. But it was the full-calf tube socks, holstered sidearm with just a hint of Abe's middle age paunch poking over, and battle helmet that made the ensemble classic Abe.

"Abe, now's not the time for busting balls," Finn said flatly. "Where's the rest of the team?"

"Don't know." Abe noticed Aislin's bleary eyes and settled a hard look on Finn. "What's going on? Nic looks like Medusa and Astrid looks like her puppy ran away."

"For the last time, it's *Aislin*, Abe. And if you're going to lead this team, you damn sure better know everyone's name." The words were out before he knew it. This wasn't his plan, but he plowed ahead anyway. "Honestly, what's wrong with you? Do you do it on purpose? Or are you really that thick?"

"He's a narcissist," Nic croaked.

"That's something else we need to address. Why are you constantly at each other's throats?"

"And you're nasty." Abe's voice was calm, and his squinting eyes remained locked on Finn. "Um, team lead? What are you trying to say?"

"I'm not *trying*. I *am* telling you that you'll be leading Strike Team Alpha. You'll get the details when the rest of the team shows up." Finn's expression left no room for debate.

"She tried to break me and Lucy up."

"Here we go," Nic mumbled exasperatedly.

"What? I don't understand. Who tried to break you up, and why?"

"Nic answers the who. The why has been hotly debated for years. It's the reason she makes my skin crawl, or, as you asked, why we're always at each other's throats."

"No debate. You're a moron and Lu could have done sooo much better, still could. Plus, I technically didn't try to break you two up. I simply told her the truth. And that was years ago. Let it go!"

"You did it *during* our wedding, the beginning of the ceremony. The priest didn't even get to the, *speak now or forever* blah, blah,

blah. You blurted it out at *dearly beloved.* Until that moment, I thought we were friends!"

"The wedding story? This ought to be good. Abe hasn't drudged it up for a while." Randy stopped next to Aislin with Stone on his heels. Both settled in for a protracted battle.

"What's this one about?" Gage whispered to Randy.

"Long story. I'll fill you in later."

"ENOUGH!" Finn's booming voice elicited a collective flinch. "We need to talk."

\*\*\*

"When do you deploy?" Stone asked.

"Two weeks. We start specialized training in seven days."

They stood quietly, digesting the news. Abe was stunned. The others wore expressions vacillating between shock and dread.

"Aislin is taking over Strike Team Bravo. Not only have they struggled to *coalesce,* but they don't possess the skill level demonstrated by Team Alpha. Until they're up and running, Team Alpha is top dog. Scavenging teams are solid and will report to Ann. She'll keep them in line. We need to talk about the guard teams. I have some thoughts and..."

"This is bullshit!" Abe shouted, pointing at Finn. "They abandoned you — left you for dead. They barred you from entering FOB Olmsted, AND wouldn't let you visit your sister, daughter, step... whatever. Now, because you survived... sorry, fought to survive, they reward you by sending you to New York City. Tell 'em to kiss your ass, Finn. This is your home now." Abe edged forward, his face flushed as his body visibly shook. "Don't let them send you to New York!"

Finn smiled grimly. "Passion and fierce loyalty, that's why you're team lead. And, I suspect, you'll inspire those same qualities in your team."

Randy's brow creased, then his head tilted. Were Abe's eyes misting over? "You going Rick Grimes on us?"

"Ouch," Stone whispered.

"It's dust!" Abe yelled.

"Who's Rick Grimes?" Gage asked quietly.

"Have you ever watched TV? Even once?" Stone mumbled softly.

"Okay, Abe, Randy, Stone, let's meet at Abe's house for dinner. I hear he has a stash of Swartz Foods lasagna." Finn glanced at each of them, his jaw hinged, then shut, his words interrupted by a truck rumbling in the distance.

"What's in the truck?" Unable to see over the barrier, Abe was drifting for the dead zone gate. Distracted like a puppy with a stick, his anger had evaporated.

Randy soon followed and Stone jogged to catch up.

"Hey, Three Stooges. I need confirmation. Are we meeting tonight?" It was no use. The trio had broken into a full run towards the gate.

"Go ahead," Finn responded to Gage's anticipatory stare. He was sprinting in an instant.

\*\*\*

"During their wedding, really?"

Nic grinned, but didn't look at Finn.

"You did the right thing. The man's insufferable. I'm still shocked Lu married him!"

Finn glanced at Aislin. He recognized the look. "I don't see it. Yeah, he can be a pain, and he's pushed my buttons more than once. But hate him? That seems a bit harsh. And the whole wedding thing... that's bitter cold."

"Men! You stick together like fuzz-covered glue. And, like I said, I merely told Lu the truth. Argue my timing all you want. It had to be done."

"Don't worry about us," Abe yelled from inside the double gate where the entrance to the dead zone was located. "We're just standing around, waiting on you, Helpful. Never mind we're probably attracting infected; you just take your sweet ol' time."

Finn's stride slowed and his smile widened. Abe was pacing between the gate and the point from where he yelled at Finn, and became more frantic as the truck neared.

"What's in the truck, Finn? I know you know, you know you know, everyone here knows you know. Spill it!"

Finn shrugged. "Couldn't tell you."

Abe's eyes widened and his mouth quivered. He looked at the advancing truck, then to Finn. "What's in the damn truck?"

"Patience, Grasshopper. You must learn patience."

Abe stormed back into the double gate and walked a tight circle until the truck squeaked to a stop. "What's in your truck?"

The truck driver leaned his head out the window. "Looking for Sergeant Finn."

"FINN! Haul ass before my head explodes!" Abe yelled while staring at the driver.

"Relax, I'm right here." Abe startled, he hadn't heard Finn walk up behind him. "Driver, I'm Sergeant Finn. The man dressed like a mental hospital escapee will open the gate for you. Pull through and await further instruction."

## Chapter 23

Thor's snarling bark set Jerry's nerves ablaze. His shepherd had never been wrong. Something was hiding in the dark. "What is it, boy? What's out there?" he whispered.

Thor remained focused on the tree line twenty yards away. Jerry hadn't noticed movement, but that's why he took Thor with him on patrol. If he reacted, Jerry knew to pay attention.

Thor charged forward, nearly ripping his leash from Jerry's grasp. "Heel." The command was firm and came with a sharp tug on Thor's leash. The shepherd stopped pulling, but remained rigid, and Jerry could see his bared teeth glisten in the moonlight.

His flashlight swept slowly across the tree line. Thor surged forward when he skimmed across a mature river birch. Jerry snapped the light back to the tree. Had something been standing there, or had the tree's mottled bark created an optical illusion? Thor's struggle to break for the tree line told him it hadn't been a trick of the eye.

"Victor, get the kids to the safe room, leave Becky and Pat to guard them. Meet me on the creek's west bank, by the drainage culvert. Thor's caught wind of something." He waited for Victor's confirmation, but received only static in reply.

He didn't wait or repeat his communication before charging through the woods for their small fortification. Victor never ignored his radio.

Jerry released Thor's leash. "Home," he yelled, knowing Thor would reach his family long before he would. He watched the animal's black and tan coat fade into the night. "Please, I'm begging. Let them be alive!"

Air exploded from his lungs the same instant his feet left the ground. Hard packed soil raced toward him as he tried to pull oxygen into his lungs. A sputtering cough racked his body when his back slammed to the earth. His legs scrabbled for purchase. He had to stand, to get to his family, but he couldn't move his arms.

His legs twisted as his back arched. The musty, earthen stench tinged with rot wasn't from woodland decay but from the beast whose jaws had just latched onto his throat.

\*\*\*

Sampson cut through the brush at a pace he would have never achieved with his soldiers in tow. The animal's pained howling drove him to the clearing which led to the paved road. Once there, he'd be able to move unencumbered by the dense growth of the woodlands and restart his search for stocked hunting grounds.

His belly was full, but the scent that struck him as he broke from the undergrowth stirred his desire. The fighter!

## Chapter 24

Archer leaned heavily against the Humvee. The handful of Ibuprofen they'd scavenged from a ransacked CVS was only successful in tearing his stomach to shreds. If he lived through the back pain, the ulcer he was working on would surely kill him.

"Alright, Gimpy, we're an hour from our target. This is our last rest stop. Make it count. I have to take a leak and search that house for food. That should give you a solid twenty to stretch. If things go sideways, yell, then lock yourself in the Hummer."

Archer struggled to turn his head toward Blum and gave a slight nod. From over Blum's shoulder, he noticed the house his travel partner was planning to search. He held little hope they'd be eating anything until they arrived at Blum's secretive target, if even then.

The classic farmhouse sat on a low rise in the middle of a barren and long forgotten field, approximately twenty yards from the gravel shoulder. The land bore the scars of heavy cultivation — corn, if he were to wager a guess. But, judging by its haggard clapboard, broken windows, and rusted farm equipment, it hadn't produced a crop in years — long before the infected slithered from Hell's gates.

"Old timers canned the food they grew," Blum answered Archer's doubtful expression. "We could get lucky."

Archer watched Blum leave the road's shoulder, traverse the slight decline which edged the home's property line, and step behind a small cluster of bushes. "Stop looking at me! I can't go if you're watching!" he yelled after making eye contact with Archer.

"Sorry, I forgot you're a timid tinkler." Archer chuckled until the shooting pain down his right leg ended his levity.

When Blum emerged from the brush, he glanced at Archer, spun a slow circle with his rifle tucked to his shoulder searching for threats, then cut a hurried path toward the house. Archer waited until the soldier reached the farmhouse porch before he gripped the front wheel well, and began a shuffling hand over hand trek to the door. Using the hood latch, side-view mirror, and any other lip, edge, or knob for support, he made it to the door and pulled it open while also using it to support his beleaguered frame.

He didn't hear the rustling brush on the far side of the roadway. But his head swiveled when the snap of a twig pierced the quiet. He tried to lift his right leg, then his left, but abandoned both attempts when the pain threatened to drop him to the pavement.

The brush began to shudder, and he could hear the low growl of a stalking monster. He gripped the door and spun his body. His triceps flexed under his weight as they hauled his body up and onto the rough canvas seat cushion.

Archer wiped away the stinging sweat running freely into his eyes. His chest heaved. He wasn't safe, not yet. He yelled for Blum as he cradled his legs and swung them into the Humvee. But the door mocked him from its fully open position. Again, he yelled for

Blum, then leaned out as far as he dared. His fingers brushed against the door, but couldn't find purchase. The brush line shook violently. Whatever hunted him was ready to charge.

"Blum! The whole world has gone sideways! Get your ass over here!" Archer flailed his hands, searching for Blum's sidearm, but couldn't find it. Leaves exploded from the bush; the monster had launched its attack. He closed his eyes and waited for gnashing teeth to tear him apart.

"Who's a good boy? Oh, you're such a pretty boy! It's okay, you're safe, you good boy, you."

Archer startled. Who the hell was Blum talking to? Was he taunting an infected?

"Look, I got some yummy jerky for you. It's stale, but you'll love it. Come on, don't be afraid. We won't hurt the pretty boy."

Archer slowly opened his eyes, uncertain of what he'd find. "Holy... where'd he come from?"

"The bushes. Didn't you, good boy?" Blum was kneeling, his hand extended, holding a hunk of dried meat. The shepherd held its ground, but its will was faltering with every flattering remark Blum heaped on it. Archer suspected Blum's singsong tone didn't hurt.

"Where'd you get the jerky?"

"Always check old farmhouses. Those people knew how to survive just about any natural disaster. Bank foreclosures, not so much."

The dog finally caved and carefully took Blum's offering. "Good boy. Where's your people? A pup as pretty as you can't be all alone." Blum took in the dog's matted fur tangled with countless twigs and travel debris. "You've got some miles on you, don't you, good boy?"

The shepherd moved in, nuzzling Blum and sniffing for more jerky. "Look at you, ya big lover. What's your name?" Blum spun the dog's collar. "Thor is a fitting name for... We gotta go. Thor, come."

Archer flinched when Blum slammed his door, then led Thor into the back seat. His rapid change in posture meant one thing.

"What'd you see?"

Blum held up his bloody hand in response. "It's smeared down his side. His people are dead. We're not waiting to see who killed them."

Archer gritted his teeth against the sudden acceleration. "I can't take much more."

"Hold on, brother. We're getting close." Blum stole a glance at Archer. The man was in trouble.

"You are a good boy, aren't you?" Blum smiled. Thor, from atop the drive train hump, had rested his head on Archer's shoulder.

## Chapter 25

Abe's head tilted right, then left, reading the block font stenciled on the line of hard-shelled crates fronting the container. "What's a MOPP? I've never heard of a weapon called MOPP. Whatever it is, I hope they sent ammo."

The truck had offloaded the cargo container in Finn's driveway, and Abe had been staring into it ever since. "How much longer, Finn?"

"When my squad shows up, you can play with the military equipment. But, to answer your question, MOPP stands for Mission Oriented Protective Posture. Think combat biohazard suits worn over BDUs. Terrible to fight in."

"These aren't the supplies we were expecting. We need weapons, not these, these MOPP thingies."

"Not for you. Command sent them ahead of our mission prep so we can acclimatize to wearing them during our training here."

Nic and Aislin gasped, understanding reached them simultaneously. "I thought you were searching for patient zero. Why are they wrapping you up in these suits? Where are they *really* sending you?"

"Don't lie, you know I'll know if you lie!" Aislin stepped next to Nic as she warned Finn.

From over Nic's shoulder, Abe smiled at Finn, taunting him. "Well, Helpful, answer Nic's question."

"We're going to New York," Finn blurted, his tone a mixture of defensiveness and confusion. "The suits serve dual roles. They'll protect us during physical infected contact."

Finn fell silent and stared at the women who had become sack-shrinkingly intimidating.

"And?" Nic barked.

"And what?"

"You said dual roles. You identified one role. We're missing a role!"

"And keep infectious agents off our skin." The explanation shot from Finn's mouth like a machinegun.

Nic edged closer to Finn, so close he could see the veins in her eyes. "Why would that be a concern, *Helpful*?"

Aislin inched next to Nic, her features as hard as the woman's whose breath caressed his chin.

Abe glanced at Randy, Stone, and Gage. Their attention pinned to the unfolding drama. He repositioned next to them, never taking his eyes off Finn. "Who throws the first punch?"

"He looks like he's getting ready to tuck tail," Randy whispered.

"We don't know what we're dealing with," Finn began as he shuffled backwards. "CENTCOM and the JCS are simply exercising an abundance of caution."

"From the looks of it, you'll be safer in New York!"

"I believe that to be an accurate statement, Abe."

Donovan appeared at the opposite side of the container with Robins and Billings in tow. "Sergeant, are you in need of an emergency EXFIL?"

"He's going to need a cast and stitches," Nic interjected. "Seems Sergeant *Helpful* likes to play fast and loose with important information."

Nobody spoke, and Finn didn't dare flinch. "We'll talk more tonight; Aislin and I have some questions." Finn recoiled when Nic brought her hand up, then ran it through her hair. "Relax, Sergeant Helpful. If I was going to throw hands, you'd already be on the ground. Now, show us what's in the container."

\*\*\*

Abe's hope faltered with each MOPP suit carried from the container. This couldn't be all they sent, could it? Hell, he could make one of these damn suits using the canvas tarp he had stashed in the garage. And why so many? Finn's squad totaled four men. They'd unloaded ten so far.

"Little help," Robins called from inside the container.

Abe went rigid. The boxes the MOPPs were packed in were heavy, but easy enough for one person to carry. He looked at Randy, then Stone, and dipped his head toward the container.

Robins stumbled against a stack of crates as the trio rushed his position. "We got this, Robins..." Abe trailed off, his eyes doe-like as he stared at the crates behind Robins. "It's beautiful... just so beautiful."

\*\*\*

Abe paced in front of the half a dozen hard plastic cases they'd unloaded. "It's a start," he said, loud enough for Finn to hear from inside the container. "When will they deliver the rest?"

"The rest?" Finn grunted as he and Donovan struggled with a large, white crate.

"I see two dozen battle rifles, four light machineguns, a couple sniper rifles — not Barrett fifty cals, I'll add — and ammo. So, yeah, where's the rest?"

"Again, Abe, the rest?"

"The Javelin Weapons Systems, mortars, hand grenades, the *rest* of the stuff!"

Finn helped Donovan hoist the white crate to the bed of Randy's truck and squared off with Abe. "Never going to happen. Now, go help Robins with the medical supplies. We need to get them to the clinic A-SAP."

"Clinic? What clinic?" Abe's confusion deepened as he met the bewildered stares of every single person unloading the container. "What?"

"Jesus H, Abe. Where the hell have you been? We talked about setting up the clinic every day during training. Jerry Green's a paramedic and his wife, Lydia, is a nurse. We converted the Zimmerman's house about a week ago."

"Jerry who? And stop talking to me like a child, Randy. I didn't know we had a clinic. Maybe I wasn't around when the topic came up?"

"Or, more likely, you didn't listen."

"Or, even *more likely*, you all failed to keep me informed! I hope you'll do better when we're outside the gate. As team leader, I expect to be updated, kept in the loop, and briefed on everything!"

Finn stepped toward Abe. It was time for a public dress-down, but the alarm blaring from the southeast watch tower froze him an instant before the entire team bolted for the tower.

"Tower, report!"

"Sergeant, a Humvee was traveling north on Ocelot, approaching the rear gate. It slowed, reversed, and disappeared down Flume. Sir, it never made it to the intersection of Flume and Day. The son of a bitch stopped somewhere in-between."

Finn nodded. "Good job... who am I speaking to?"

"John Whitaker, sir. I have the intersection of Ocelot and Flume covered. Request permission to engage if they approach?"

"Negative, Whitaker. Hold until we arrive. Stay low and vigilant. We'll be there in two."

The tower came into view as Finn broke contact with Whitaker. He couldn't see the guard, but knew where he'd find him.

"Combat distance. Take covered positions at the base of the tower. Call out any visuals and wait for my orders. Break, now!" Finn hit the staircase as the team fanned out below. With only sidearms, they were unprepared for a sustained direct assault — he prayed they'd avoid bloodshed.

"Last visual?" Finn held Whitaker's binoculars to his eyes and waited.

"Blue house, third from the intersection."

Finn focused on that location and observed the gaps to its left and right. The vehicle would have been highly visible traveling in either direction. "You're sure?"

"Absolutely."

"Donovan, Billings, retrieve your gear and return to the tower. I want your guns with Whitaker's covering the intersection. The rest of you gear up and meet at the rear gate. Radio me when you arrive and I'll link up at that point. Aislin, bring my kit with you. MOVE!"

A thought punched Finn as he watched the house. "Finn for foot patrol."

"This is Smith."

"Smith, what's you force size?"

"Four, sir."

"Send two to reinforce the main gate guards and two to reinforce the rear gate. All towers, stay alert. Call out visual contacts and wait for my orders. This may be a diversion."

Finn nodded as the confirmations rolled in. This could get sticky, but they sounded determined. "Don't piss with us," he growled.

## Chapter 26

"Take cover and keep your heads on swivels," Finn told the guards as the smaller rear entrance's double gate closed behind them. "You hear gunfire, hold position and radio Ann for backup. She's aware of the situation and has boots standing by."

Finn spun on his heel and set course toward their target's last known location. He glanced over his shoulder. His team was in wedge formation, at six-foot intervals. They'd listened to him! "Until we make contact, we are radio silent!"

They had a hundred yards of coverless land to traverse before they reached the hedgerow behind the target house. The urge to run, to get his team behind cover, was tickling the base of his skull. *Slow is fast, fast is slow.*

At twenty yards, he called a stop with a raised fist, stuck four fingers in the air, and waved it at the intersection. Nic, Aislin, Robins and Gage moved past him, angling for a raised flowerbed skirting the lawn of the first house. Four fingers went up again and waved at the hedgerow.

Finn led the way through the overgrowth. His team was silent; even in full battle rattle they understood maintaining stealth was imperative. He twirled his hand above his head and brought his team in tight. "Donovan, do you have visuals?" Finn's whisper was barely audible.

"Negative."

"Robins, does your team have visuals?"

"Affirmative. Up-armored Humvee with possibly two combatants visible. Vehicle is not running. Facing north on the west side of the target house. Hold..."

Finn leaned forward, waiting for Robins to continue. "We have movement inside target."

"Clarify movement."

"Nic reported drape movement."

"Roger. Hold position and put muzzles on that window and the windows across the street."

Finn glanced at his team. They hadn't taken their eyes off him since leaving the gate. His gaze lingered on Abe. The man was as still and quiet as he'd ever seen him — it was unnatural, and made it impossible to read his emotional state.

"Well, boys. We're about to test our training. Randy, you're with me. We're breaching. Abe, Stone, you take the Humvee. When you hear the door breach, move on the vehicle's left and right flanks. It's armored, so your goal is to contain the enemy. Move out."

"One question." Finn cringed as Abe continued. "Why didn't we approach in our Humvees? I'm assuming you expected an ambush and wanted to avoid losing them to enemy fire?"

Finn's eyebrows arched. Abe's assumption was dead nuts. Their Humvees weren't up-armored, even a novice with an RPG could end every life inside. "Affirmative, Abe. Now, let's roll."

Abe grinned. This soldiering stuff came second nature. "Follow my lead, brother. I got this."

Finn waited until Abe and Stone clicked their radios, confirming they were in position.

"On three, Randy."

"Got it, on three."

Finn caught Randy's foot mid-flight and held it tight so the man didn't tumble to his rear-end and give away their position. "You've got to get better at that," Finn whispered. "Now, watch my fingers. When three are up, kick the door.

Randy ignored the moisture tickling his cheeks and focused solely on Finn's hand. His foot crashed into the door when Finn's third finger popped up.

"Stay in the vehicle!" Abe shouted as Stone did the same. Their approach was swift, as each moved in a fighting crouch.

"I've got one. He appears wounded," Stone called out.

"I've got a, uh, a *puppy*. Who's a good *boy*?"

"Focus, Abe. Backseat appears clear. Target is not moving, may be dead."

"Backseat is clear. Beautiful puppy is highly agitated."

Glass pelted Stone's back. He spun to find Randy floating through the air with an unidentified soldier held tight to his chest. Finn appeared in the shattered picture window as Randy slammed the enemy to the lawn.

"Stop struggling!" Randy huffed as he fought against the squirming soldier.

"You stop, Randy."

Randy froze. "How do you know my name?" He pulled back from their tangle and smiled. "Jay! Holy crap. I almost killed you. What are you doing? Why didn't you come to the gate?

Abe angled around the Humvee's brush guard and past his gawking brother. His rifle remained at high ready. "Randy, what are you doing?"

"Relax, Abe. It's Jay Blum."

"Who? And if he's friendly, why was he hiding, setting up an ambush?"

"Hey, Mister Willings," Blum said as Randy pulled him to his feet with a grunt. "To be honest, the militarization of the neighborhood spooked me. I wasn't sure if you all abandoned it and a bunch of whack jobs took over."

"Sergeant Blum! You're shitting me!" Finn bellowed as he leapt from the window. "Last I heard... well, you know what I heard."

"Finn? Shamus Finn! Holy..." Blum stopped talking as he rushed to embrace his former squad leader. "Yeah, the stories of my demise have been greatly exaggerated." He pulled away from Finn. He was smiling for the first time in over a month.

"Who the hell are you?" Abe shouted, his rifle only marginally lower.

"I lived across the street from you. Ann's my mom. You used to yell at me for hitting my baseballs into your yard... you kept them, every time."

*Ann has a kid?* Abe lowered his rifle. He still didn't know the soldier, but the relaxed posture of the people around him eased his intensity.

"Jay! Good to see you!" Gage yelled as his squad approached from their hide.

"Can I see your pup?" Abe asked, distracted by the snarling shepherd.

"Oh, shit. That reminds me. We've got to get my friend to a doctor. It's a long story, but he's in terrible shape. As for the pup. He doesn't seem to like you, Abe. I only just found him, but he's been calm — up till now."

"Nah, dogs love me."

Randy snickered. Everyone who knew Abe was convinced his last words would be, *oh look, a puppy.*

"We can worry about the dog later. Let's get your friend to our clinic, and you to your mom. I'm sure she'll be happy to see you."

"Finn, did the DoD contact her?"

"Not that I'm aware. But they've been struggling. Let's get things buttoned up, then we'll talk."

Blum was still smiling when he fired up the Humvee. He was home, and his people were alive.

***

Three days had passed, but the excitement viewed through the binoculars and arrival of another soldier dictated more time was needed. A rummage through the backpack made clear that three days of food remained. Another three days it would be.

# Chapter 27

Abe pounded on Ann's front door until Lu answered. "Are you trying to get yourself killed?" she hissed. "You're lucky I beat Ann to the door!"

"They sent me because they know I'll aggravate her. You're ruining their plan."

"Who is they and what plan? I'm stuck with her all..." Lu trailed off. "Is that..."

Abe shushed Lu by putting a finger to his lips. "Ann," he yelled. "Don't hide from me, woman. We need to talk — right now!"

"Lucy, you have fifteen seconds to get that man off my property!"

"Hey, woman! I'm talking to you, not Lu. Now get out here. We need to talk about your feelings for me. We both know fighting our raw attraction is futile. Come give this man some love!"

Abe backpedaled as Ann approached spewing expletives when she caught sight of him. Lu rushed through the door as the matriarch hit the threshold. "I swear on all things holy I'm going to wrap my hands around your scrawny neck and squeeze the life from your vile body. Although, that obviously wouldn't work because I was praying that whoever was in that Hummer would kill you!"

Ann's pace quickened in time with Abe's retreat, her crimson visage twisted as she closed the gap between them.

"Mom."

Ann shook her head, her legs went rubbery, but she continued to move forward. "Mom, I'm home."

Abe stepped aside and let Jay pass. Ann's eyes filled with tears, her mouth moved but said nothing. She took another step before her legs folded, but her gaze never faltered.

"Mom!" Jay exclaimed, as he rushed to kneel beside her.

Ann cupped his face in her hands. Her eyes searched his as her hands caressed his scruffy cheeks. "My boy, oh my boy is home," she sobbed. The world and its horrors faded; her son was alive.

Lu held a hand to her mouth. Her shoulders trembled as the reunion blurred. She wiped the moisture from her eyes and fought the urge to embrace them. But this was their moment and she dared not intrude.

She leaned into Abe, and he pulled her in tight. "I don't remember Ann having a kid?" he whispered.

Lu didn't answer, she was still watching Ann.

"We should leave them alone," Abe said, while gently turning her. "But seriously, how long has she had him?"

***

Finn followed Abe's Irish exit and grabbed Nic's hand. He left Blum's Humvee parked in the street. The walk to the clinic would do him good and hopefully distract Nic.

"Do you have to go?" she asked, her voice cracking with emotion.

He pulled her in and kissed her. "I do. We can end this."

Nic buried her head in his chest. "I can hear your heart. Promise you'll bring it back to me."

Finn kissed the top of her head and held her. He couldn't make that promise.

***

Thor greeted Finn and Nic at the entrance, sniffed them, and moved aside, allowing them to enter.

"He's been doing that since you dropped him and Archer off," Jerry said in answer to their bemused looks. "Must be the breed. He's protecting Archer, but he needs a bath."

Thor groaned mournfully and scampered down the hall. "With all he's probably been through, it's a bath he's afraid of!" Jerry shook his head as he watched the shepherd disappear into Archer's room.

"How's he doing?" Finn asked.

"As best we can tell, he's either herniated a disc or fractured his spine. His gradual physical deterioration speaks to herniation. We have him on a morphine drip, but he's going to need surgery. In addition to shooting pain, he's lost the use of his right leg. We've done what we can, but, like I said, he needs surgery."

Finn met Jerry's gaze, then answered the unasked question. "I'll radio Olmsted and ask if they have a surgeon. When will it be safe to move him?"

"The man just traveled several hundred miles in a Hummer. Safe isn't a worry. He just needs some rest, but should be ready for transport by morning. We'll juice him up before you leave."

Finn turned when the door opened behind them. "Abel?"

"What? I wanted to check on, on... the pilot guy. How is he? I was thinking, Thor probably needs a walk. Poor guy's been cooped up for God knows how long."

Jerry's head snapped toward the hallway, drawn by a low growl. "Well, he hasn't done that before. What's wrong, boy?"

Thor stalked forward, his teeth glistened as his hackles rose.

"See, he needs a walk. Come here, Thor. Uncle Abe's going to take you on a nice long walk."

"Holy sh..." Jerry shouted as he spun out of Thor's way.

"Run," Finn shouted and pushed Abe out the door and slammed it an instant before Thor crashed into it.

Thor recovered from the impact and paced in front of the door, growling in between snarling barks.

"Abe, Thor doesn't seem to like you," Finn shouted. "You should go. You're upsetting him and there are sick people in here. They need to rest."

Thor went ridged at the sound of the doorknob turning. Finn grabbed Nic's hand and pulled it from the knob. "Not cool, Nic!"

"No, but it would be fun to watch."

"Okay, I'll head home and check back tomorrow. He's probably hungry. He'll be in a better mood after he eats. I'll bring him some snacks. Cuz he's a *good boy*."

Thor scratched at the door while Abe talked. He didn't stop until Abe was on the street, walking home.

# Chapter 28

Sampson peered down at the sprawling building. The moonless night perfect for hunting, his position on the hillside ideal for savoring the aroma. *Hundreds are hiding there.*

He crouched low into the field grass as the fighter's lights swept across the hillside. The defenses here appeared stronger than those in the city where Su was destroyed.

Again, he inhaled. The air was rich with fear, fueling his desire to feed. But the fighters were vigilant, and immeasurable. Their machines crept along the fence with blinding lights and vicious weapons. More walked the expanse between the fence and the walls housing the food. He needed soldiers. He would find soldiers.

He waited for the nearest machine to pass, then slithered through the grass to the hill's crest where he faded into the night.

Sampson darted through the dark; these lands were ripe with food and fighters. His head tilted as a warm breeze, carrying a familiar scent, rustled his matted hair. Through vacant lots and abandoned playgrounds, it guided him. Some of his were close.

\*\*\*

"Jenney, I need your assistance in my workshop. Come quickly."

The young woman recoiled. What remained of their original group feared Stanley's workshop. It always seemed to be the last place each of the eight missing members of their group were seen.

"I'm, uh, I'm on guard duty, Stanley. Can it wait until morning?" Jenney wrung her hands together and paced the expansive living room, cursing the others for leaving her behind while they went scavenging. She had pleaded with them to allow her to join them, but it was her turn for guard duty. *Guard what?* She had argued, *he forbids us from having weapons, or walking the grounds. We merely sit in the window with a warning bell!* They had ignored her plea, all too happy to escape the grounds, and face the dangers of an infected world. Even if only for an hour, they'd be free of the oppressive atmosphere Stanley had fostered.

"We are secure — for the moment." Jenney screamed when she heard his voice, not realizing he had entered the room.

"My, my, aren't you a Nervous Nelly? Now, as I was saying, we are secure and my research is critical. Please," he stepped in her direction, his right hand hidden from sight, "come with me."

***

Sampson held his face to the breeze. The familiar scent was overpowering. Why hadn't he seen them? His hands gripped the low black fence, but ripped free as his body jolted backwards.

He clawed at his neck, but the cable seemed to have melted into his skin. He twisted sharply, but couldn't break free.

"My, my, you're a fighter."

Sampson tried to pivot — the voice was directly behind him.

"You must be hungry. I've never had one of you fight like this. I'll feed you if you cooperate."

Sampson stilled. Had this man offered him food?

"You understood what I said," the man gasped.

Sampson allowed his shoulders to slump. He'd played this game before. This man was a do-gooder trying to assuage his conscience by feeding the wretched soul, begging for his change. It would end for him as it had the others Sampson had encountered when he lived on the streets.

"I knew you were still human, all of you! I can help you regain your humanity. Your path to redemption starts here. Now march!"

Sampson lurched forward, his captor in control of his steps.

\*\*\*

"Oh dear, I had hoped this part would be over before I returned. I do hate watching." Stanley forced his new subject to the back of an open cage, fed the control pole through the feed slot, released the Velcro strap securing his right hand to the pole, slammed the cage shut, and released the cable's tension, freeing his subject. He braced for its violent reaction, but the infected remained still, his eyes searching the surroundings.

"You're thinking, aren't you? I've been seeking one like you. You hold the key!" The man glanced over his shoulder. "I apologize for the squalid conditions. My work often requires... shall I say, a few eggs be broken."

The man stepped back, admiring his subject, then approached the cage and slid his hand through the feed slot. "I'm Stanley, Stanley Chatham."

Sampson's head tilted, glaring at the man who'd unwittingly offered him a sample of his flesh. He remained still. He was trapped and the do-gooder offered his only chance of escape. Eating him would ensure he never fed again.

"Not there, yet? I understand. You're probably still disgruntled about the way I secured your capture. I implore your understanding. The use of the animal control pole is a necessary evil. Your kind seems more interested in eating me than with healing. It affords me a superior amount of leverage..."

Stanley spun as a scream rose above the chaos of dozens of feeding infected. "Oh my, how did that happen?" he mumbled as he scurried away from Sampson's cage. "I applied an exceptional amount of duct tape. It should have held until they finished with you."

"STOP! You sick bastard! How can you do this? You're not curing anything, you're not even a scientist. Please, I'm begging, stop!"

Stanley ignored the woman and retrieved a roll of tape from his workbench and tore a two-foot piece free. "Now, try not to wriggle free of this one, Jenney." He grasped a handful of the woman's hair and pulled her head forward, wrapped the silver strip around her matted hair and cheeks stained black from mascara, and covered her mouth. "Your screeching will only increase as they feed. I find it unsettling, which is why I had hoped they'd have finished by the time I returned." Stanley stared into her wide, damp eyes. She didn't understand how important she was. "Those I cure will honor your contribution to my work. Try to embrace your inner strength and accept your extraordinary fortune. Children will read about you and lift your name in song."

Her body jerked and shuttered as he released her head. The infected on the other side of the cage increased their feeding. They tugged on her exposed flesh through the diamond shaped openings in the cage. He found this method allowed the meal to last longer, affording the weaker subjects an opportunity to gain nourishment. The infected also seemed to *enjoy* their meals more when the feedstock struggled to free themselves.

His subjects developed an understanding of the process, and, by the third feeding, stopped trying to bite through his thick, leather dog training gloves as he strapped the feedstock to the cage. They had seemed prone to attack during the application of the shoulder and hip straps, never the ankle straps. He'd noted the anomaly in his journal, as he had the other oddities he'd observed.

Satisfied he'd silenced Jenney, Stanley reengaged with his new subject. It had moved to the front of his cage, its eyes watching the others feed.

"I did indeed ply you with the promise of a meal. You'll learn Stanley Chatham is a man of his word. Give me a moment." Stanley reached for the machete tethered to the post next to

Sampson's cage. "I'll return shortly with your meal. After which, our work begins."

## Chapter 29

Blum pushed deep into his chair. Finn had finished his update and he decided he'd have been better off staying on the road.

"Anyway, the CO at FOB Olmsted wants to meet with you. It's going to be your standard after action review. And you have every right to refuse. My squad, and dozens like it, were also abandoned. But you — they tried to kill you and slaughtered your men."

"When are you transporting Archer?"

"Today. Why, you want us to hold off, give you time to mull it over? He can probably hold tight for another day, but no longer. Plus, the CO didn't time stamp your arrival. You can go whenever you want."

Blum sat forward and glanced around. "Do you know where my mom is?"

"She's with Lu. They're canvassing the community, looking for people with useful skills. We need a lot of roles filled."

Blum smiled. "Mom knows what everyone does... it's her thing. I promise, they've only gone to homes where they'll find what they need. If she suddenly appears next to me, I'll stop talking and you'll know why." He glanced over his shoulder. "I'll go with you today. Archer needs a doctor and transporting him will be a good excuse for me to go to Olmsted. She doesn't need to know every detail of the trip."

Finn chuckled. "Yeah, I understand." He paused, then pushed forward. Blum had to know what to expect. "Like I said, they're going to try to recruit you, get ready for the hard sell routine. The big green machine is stretched pretty thin. They're looking for Grunts who fought their way out of certain death. I'd say you fit that description."

"Just don't mention it to my mom. At least not until I know what I'm doing."

The lights flickered, then leveled off. "That's been happening more and more this week. Kinda proves my point about how thin things are getting. Power goes — morale goes with it."

"PA is dark, well, most of it. The darker it got, the fewer people I saw. I'm sure my mom's working that angle — looking for someone to keep the lights on."

Finn rested his arms on the table and inched forward until it dug into his stomach. "I have a question. Seems insignificant considering the shit show we're dealing with, and you'll probably think I'm a moron for asking. But I gotta know. What did Lieutenant Sanchez tell you guys about me? Why I didn't deploy that second time?"

"Surprisingly, the prick acted human for once. He told us about your family and what you were doing. He actually admitted your boots would be hard to fill. I was disappointed I wouldn't get more time with you. You taught me a lot during our first deployment. The shit they don't teach in basic."

Blum watched Finn's chest relax. What his old squad thought of him meant something to him.

"Well, you were a quick study — for a green weenie. I'll never forget your baby face stepping off that transport the same instant they hit us with that eight-one mortar. But you moved, listened to orders and kept your wits. And, thanks. I figured he'd trash me. It's good to know he didn't."

Blum was the fourth of his former squad mates he'd asked about Sanchez. They'd all relayed the same story. But he'd always worry. It was how he was wired.

"Alright," Finn said, while pushing back from the table, "let's secure Archer, and get this outta the way."

***

"You've been home not even twenty-four hours! I haven't seen you in months. Slide your ass out of that, that monstrosity and go home!"

"Mom! We've got an injured man in here. He's my friend and I'm going with him," Blum yelled from the Humvee's passenger window. "Move away from the gate and let us pass. I'll be home in a few hours."

Ann stepped closer to the Humvee's brush guard and locked her glare on Finn. "And you! Who do you think you are, taking my son away from me? What did you tell him? I know my boy. He wouldn't abandon me unless *someone* filled his head with a bunch of crap!"

"Help me out, Jay. Your mom's a scary woman."

Thor whimpered from the vehicle's slant back cargo hold. He was guarding Archer, but appeared rattled by Ann's forceful objection to Blum traveling through the gate. "I'm with ya, boy," Finn whispered as the standoff continued.

"Mom... Jesus, you're embarrassing me. I have to go. It's important."

"What's the base commander's name?" Ann asked as she approached the passenger side window and ripped a notepad from her breast pocket.

"Go!" Blum yelled when his mom cleared from their path.

Finn trounced on the accelerator, heaving them through the gate.

"She's going to be *pissed*."

"Brother, you don't know the half of it."

\*\*\*

Lieutenant Richards, of FOB Olmsted, tapped his laptop's *enter* button. A moment later, the JCS, minus General Malloy, filled the overhead monitor.

"Place didn't look like this when I went to school here," Blum mumbled, referring to the commandeered high school and its grounds that comprised Forward Operating Base Olmsted.

The base, a sprawling multistory complex surrounded by acres of land, now bustled with soldiers, military families, medical staff, and the machines of war. Olive drab shelters ringed the school where hundreds more civilians were being housed on churned earth. The neighboring middle school, approximately half the high school's size, was being readied to become a secondary housing unit. It appeared the Forward Operating Base moniker would soon be dropped, and the complex would simply be referred to as Camp Olmsted. This war had no end in sight.

"Gentlemen," Richards said, "I'm here with Sergeants Blum and Finn. I have something I want to address before we move forward..."

Malloy's entrance stifled Richards. "I apologize for the disruption. Please, Lieutenant, continue."

Blum's head snapped to Finn. He didn't know Malloy had joined the JCS. "What the hell?" he whispered. "When did that happen?"

"Sergeant Blum, at the LT's indulgence, I'll field that question before we move forward."

Richards nodded his approval, then turned to Blum and Finn.

"I share your shock that I'm the Chairman of the Joint Chiefs. It's a testament to the speed and savagery with which the infection has spread. And, when leadership is lost in battle, they'll tap any gray-haired idiot with stars on his shoulder to fill vacant roles."

A chuckle rippled through the Joint Chiefs members before Malloy continued. "Sergeant, I cannot express adequately the regret I harbor for the action taken against your men and for abandoning you in Central Park. When we talked and I informed you of the Pentagon's updated ROEs, your reaction was that of a soldier. A true warrior. I'm not going to beg your forgiveness, because, frankly, I don't deserve to be forgiven. I failed you and hundreds like you and deserve to relive that shame every time I stare into the eyes of the soldiers we left behind."

Blum sensed Finn's eyes on him. "You couldn't have known, Finn."

The silence stood on Blum's chest. He had no grand statements, none that would change what had happened. "I'll honor your wishes, General."

The slightest of grins tugged Malloy's lips. "Very good. Richards, please continue."

The LT cleared his throat. "During our after action review, Sergeant Blum shared what I believe to be previously unknown INTEL. The infected are afraid of fire. They'll eventually attack, but only after being held at bay and in the absence of easier prey. Also, he and Captain Archer, on separate occasions, witnessed *fights* break out between opposing infected factions. This stands counter to the intelligence we received regarding cooperative hunting."

Malloy sat forward, his brows heavy with concern. "Fighting? Sergeant Blum, have you reviewed the target packages?"

Blum shook his head. Malloy's reaction surprised him. He'd assumed the information regarding fire held greater value.

"Holy shit!" Blum shouted when two faces flashed onto the monitor. "I've seen the scraggly one identified as Sampson. Had the SOB dead to rights in Central Park, but he got away. I can tell you, he's not in New York. He dogged me across Pennsylvania. He's a crafty bastard. Drop a team at the Ohio Pennsylvania state line. Last time I saw him, he was charging into the brush, trying to escape from the fire we'd set. That was a hell of a fire. Chances are you'll only find his corpse."

Blum squinted at the second face. He'd only seen this monster from a distance, and wanted to be certain it was the same man he'd viewed through his binoculars. He dipped his head sharply.

"The other was also in Central Park. He and Sampson squared off. I can't give you a disposition. But I'd start your search there." Blum paused. "Sir, what I'm about to say may sound crazy. The targets, both of them, seemed to be *communicating*. Their eyes... something about them spoke to intelligence. And the other infected seemed to be loyal to either Sampson or Su. Not both."

Malloy glared at Colonel Rey, who remained focused on the monitor. "Sergeant, you detected intelligence because they possess, at a rudimentary level, the ability to reason, to think. I was late for our meeting due to a DARPA update. There had been speculation that the infection, or fungus, had hijacked their hosts' bodies and destroyed all but their brain's basic functions. DARPA now believes the fungus allowed the brain to live, and worked with its host. That's why they exhibited cognitive abilities far beyond what you'd expect from an individual with, let's say, traumatic brain injuries. However, with each successive *generation,* and as they age, the fungus gains more control, becomes more aggressive, and seeks to obtain whatever its goals are, at all costs. So, it's very possible they were communicating, but that ability has become virtually nonexistent. Nevertheless, their need to feed on human flesh has increased."

Blum ran a hand down his face. He was a soldier, not a scientist, and he'd obviously been unclear. "Sir, they were communicating, but they weren't talking."

## Chapter 30

Abe watched their movements, or lack thereof, through his binoculars. They'd wedged themselves between the house and the extended cab pickup truck, taking the Humvee's brush guard out of the fight. The trailer was still hitched to the truck and sat heavy with supplies — they needed everything on that trailer.

They'd received word that the scavenging team's mission had gone sideways, and geared up in the middle of training. Abe had them rolling through the gate in a matter of minutes. With Finn and Blum at FOB Olmsted, the rest of Finn's squad drilling in their MOPPs, and using a different channel, Abe made the call. This was their mission, their people to save.

"Bobby, do you have eyes on the backyard?"

Randy glanced at Stone; Abe remembered the man's name.

"We've split to cover all sides, just like we were trained."

"Good man. Are they only in front of the house, or have they surrounded you?"

"Front and west side. Abel, they could have easily entered the house by now. What are they doing?"

"Honestly, I don't know. And there's no time to figure it out. Hold tight, we're going to get you out of there. When I tell you to move, you move. Clear?"

"Crystal."

Abe switched his coms off and signaled the team to follow suit.

"Who's engaging?" Randy asked.

"Since you're driving, you are. Stone, you're with me. Gage, Nic, when Randy pulls next to the pickup, open fire. Mind your lines, our people are trapped on the second floor. Once you have their attention, Randy will edge west while you do whatever it takes to keep them interested. But, once you're rolling, keep your fire to a minimum. Stone and I will be in the backyard, and neither of us wants to take an errant round to the chest."

Abe waited for confirmation. When none came, he set the binoculars in his lap and turned to face his team. "What?"

"You feeling alright?"

"I'm good. Why?"

"No reason. Just checking in. Let me know when you're in position. I'll advance... engage at that point."

Abe held a suspicious eye on Randy while he exited the Humvee. Stone joined him a second later. "You ready?"

"No, but Bobby sounded rattled. So, after you, Abe."

\*\*\*

"Holy shit, there's hundreds of them." Abe whispered as he and Stone peered at the herd through gaps in an overgrown thicket. "It didn't look like that many from a quarter mile away."

"Abe, have you seen their skin?"

\*\*\*

"Do you think something's wrong with him?"

Gage looked up from press-checking his Glock. "It was odd. He remembered Bobby's name, didn't crack a joke, and seemed unreasonably calm."

"Probably on valium." Nic released her M4A1's charging handle, letting the bolt carrier slam forward. "He better stay frosty. Lives are depending on him having a clear head."

"Stay frosty? Your boyfriend teach you that?"

"Shut up, Randy. I'm just saying people are counting on him. If he's doped up, someone could end up dead."

"Hammer Actual for Hammer Three." Abe's voice crackled through Randy's headset.

"Abe, who's Hammer Three?"

"You're Hammer Three. We needed call signs. I like Hammer. And it's time for Hammer Three to engage. Hammer Two and Hammer Actual will approach the target structure when the infected peel off. We'll return to base with Bobby's team."

"Hammer Three, engaging. And, Abe, you're supposed to assign call signs before a mission."

"Roger that, Hammer Three. Hammer Actual, out."

\*\*\*

"I'm not calling you Hammer Actual." Stone followed Abe through the tangle of vines and undergrowth, then shifted to his right.

"Sure you will. I mean, not when it's just you and me talking. But when the entire team has their boots on the ground, you'll be required to use call signs."

Abe's fist rose above his head, silencing Stone and halting their advance. "Hammer Three is approaching. Hug the ground."

Stone eye-rolled, but followed Abe's lead. Nic and Gage opened fire a few seconds later. Their full-auto barrage was quick and intense, followed by tirades, laced with obscenities and punctuated with threats, screamed at the infected.

"Seriously, her voice cuts like a hot knife through butter."

"I'm going with nails on a chalkboard."

"Truly awful. Can you imagine being married to that? Probably why Finn hasn't asked her to move in with him. But I'm telling you, Stone. I have to get her out of my house!"

\*\*\*

Nic stood in the open backdoor's frame and screamed. It wasn't until she joined Gage's verbal assault that the infected responded. Her voice proved more effective than the full magazine dumps they'd just finished.

"You want smoke? I'm bringing the smoke! You are the sorriest bunch of pus bags I've ever seen. Yeah, I'm talking to you, tiny, and you, ya fat ass!"

"They're moving in our direction."

"Abe, Gage reports movement. Stand ready."

"Hammer Three, I heard words spoken, but remain unable to verify your intended recipient."

"ABE! The infected are moving. Do what you will with the information. I'm tucked safely inside tons of steel. You... are not!"

"Roger, Hammer Three. Hammer Actual is on the move."

# The Wild Ones

***

Abe leaned against the siding and eased his head around the corner. Most of the infected had taken the bait.

He held up five fingers, then pointed in the direction of the stragglers. "Those are the only hand signals I know," Abe whispered. "They're not moving — at all. And I see what you were talking about. Their skin is all kinds of wrong."

"Bobby for Abe, SITREP?"

Abe jolted at Bobby's voice. "Jesus, Bobby. You scared the shit out of me. I told you, we'll let you know when to move. That time has *not* arrived."

Abe's right hand whirled, slapping against the house as he tried to grab Stone. His brother's confusion cleared when his eyes locked on Abe's chest an instant before he was yanked from sight.

The landscape blurred as Abe beat on the monster's arm, trying to wrench free of its grip. "What the..." his face was inches from gnashing teeth. The stench rolling from the infected's mouth stung his vision and forced burning nausea into his throat.

Another tug on his vest snapped his head and shook him from his stupor. Teeth and goo splattered in every direction as Abe's gloved fist pummeled the infected. His left hand slid to his belt. His counterattack merely keeping the infected at bay. But his arching blade ended the beast.

The monster slid from view as he sheathed his knife and shouldered his M4A1. The stragglers had scattered and were approaching from multiple angles. "Stone! Where are you?"

"Got your back. One of them flanked our six." Stone's M4A1 thundered. "I snapped his neck, but he damn near had me for lunch."

"I'm counting more than five. They sucked us in again!" Abe lined up a charging infected and stroked the trigger, but it had already dropped from sight, his rounds lacing a trailing monster's chest. It spun to the ground, but struggled to its feet in seconds.

Abe's trigger finger tensed, his aim dropped to the thing's hips. He didn't have to shoot. The infected seized, then fell stiffly to the grass. Its body pulsed violently, then went still. He didn't have time to investigate — more infected had taken up the charge.

"Stone, is our six clear?"

"Hold." Stone's M4A1 barked. "It is now."

"Fall back. Bobby, I need your eyes. Where are they coming from?" Abe's voice jostled as he and Stone ran towards the backyard.

Bobby's voice filled his headset. "South side of the street. Looks like a medium-sized utility shed. They're still rolling out."

"We need covering fire. Concentrate on the shed. Randy?" Abe yelled after Bobby confirmed an instant before he and his team opened fire.

"Go for Hammer Three."

Blistering gunfire filtered through Abe's headset. "SITREP?"

"Hammer Actual, things have gone a tad sideways. All the other Hammers are currently surrounded. We're pushing through now.

But several dozen of the original herd's friends have joined the party. We're at a crawl."

"When you're clear, we need an EVAC. We'll fall back and regroup."

"We're going to outrun our covering fire and the Humvee." Stone slid to a stop, spun, and emptied his magazine, spilling a handful of infected.

Abe squared up next to his brother and took up their defense as Stone reloaded.

"I didn't mean to dump that mag," he shouted as he released the charging handle and chambered a round. "Wish I had my Springfield."

Abe's battle rifle's bolt carrier locked back. "Reloading," he yelled as he dropped the empty magazine and inserted a fresh one.

\*\*\*

Randy slapped Gage's back. "Pull back and roll up your window; we're pushing through. We've got enough clearance." He reached into the back and shook Nic's leg, then signaled her to retract from the open window. She'd been covering Gage's flanks as he thinned the herd from their path.

"Hold on!" The Humvee lurched forward, pushing them into their seats, before jerking to a stop.

Randy shifted into *reverse* and gunned the accelerator. The Humvee responded by sluicing hard right before he backed off the power.

"No traction." Randy shifted into *drive,* set the transfer case to *low,* and tapped the accelerator. The Humvee's engine revved but the drive train barely responded. Nevertheless, they didn't slide and pushed forward at a snail's pace.

"Why couldn't we gain traction?" Gage asked as he peered into the side view mirror. "Are we leaking oil?"

"Don't think that's it." Randy sent more power to the whining drive train. Infected were pulled along as they clung to the brush guard; their feet scraped through the fluff and muck collecting on the pavement. Their bodies became gruesome cowcatchers, sweeping their brethren to the sides.

"Holy..." Gage trailed off, he'd caught a glimpse of the roadway behind them.

"Yeah, that's what I thought. They don't design tire treads deep enough to cut through that much gore." Randy pushed the Humvee as hard as he dared while in *low.* "When we break free, I'm going to create some space." The Humvee bounced and jostled violently, cutting Randy off.

"What the hell, Randy!" Nic yelled from the backseat, rubbing her head where it had slammed against the window.

"Infected shook free of the guard and slipped under us. Listen up, at twenty yards, we open fire. We can't lead these things back to the house. Sack up, we're almost through."

\*\*\*

Stone flared wide right, intercepting a gaggle of infected while Abe leveled a heavily damaged man who'd accelerated rapidly to within three yards of their position. "Ammo?"

"One in my chest rig, half mag loaded." Abe advanced to the front of the house.

"This is my last mag. It's half, maybe less, full. What's it look like up there?" Stone swept his M4A1 over the side and backyards. "Our rear flank is clear."

"Front is clear. Stone, you gotta see this."

"Holy," Stone mumbled when he joined Abe, "what the hell's happening to them?"

Abe pulled his brother back as the infected they were scrutinizing began trembling. Its mouth opened, then stretched far beyond its limits, snapping its jaw as coal gray fluff bubbled out.

"Oh, its eyes, look at its eyes." Abe winced, his body turned sideways, but he couldn't break his stare. "Oh, that's so nasty," he shouted as white tendrils discharged the monster's eyes from their sockets. The freshly liberated orbs rode a wave of fluff down infected cheeks to the saturated earth.

The brothers took another instinctive step back, watching the tendrils race from one festering wound to another. The ghoulish roadmap they formed constricted, forcing more fluff to escape the deflating corpse until nothing solid, but its clothing, remained.

"Bobby for Abe, we clear to exit?"

Abe yelped and spun, searching for the voice's owner. "Damn it, Bobby... yes, you're clear to exit."

Bobby's team of four scavengers exited the house with their rifles tucked tightly against their shoulders and made a beeline for their truck. Abe was prepared to shout them down but held his tongue when they set up a defensive perimeter, using the truck as cover. *Finn was right, they're solid.*

"Where's Randy?" Bobby asked.

As if on cue, gunfire erupted in the distance. "Randy, SITREP?"

"Hammer Actual, this is Hammer Three. Was your SITREP request intended for me?"

Abe rubbed between his eyebrows. "SIT-REP!"

"The Hummer Hammers are mopping up. Will rally at your position in five."

"Wipe the shit-eating grin off your face and double-time your ass back to the target house."

"Sir, yes sir. The Hammers march in five."

\*\*\*

"This is bullshit," Abe shouted between retching gasps.

"We need a sample. The quicker you move, the quicker we're out of here." Stone was enjoying his brother's distress.

Abe dipped the empty water bottle into the puddle of humanity and scooped it through what had once been its head.

"Ziploc, now!" he dropped the bubbling mess into the bag and let Bobby seal it.

Wobbly on his feet, he locked his team in a worried gaze. They didn't know what was happening, only that it wouldn't end well.

"Let's go home," he said, just above a whisper.

## Chapter 31

Finn angled the brush guard for a glancing blow. His target spun from its feet and landed in a shattered heap. "I'll never get used to it. And knowing that, technically, they're still alive... that'll rattle the soul. Maybe we shouldn't share that with the community. If they let the fact that they're killing actual living people get in their heads, they may hesitate. That happens and our body count explodes."

Finn waited for Blum's input, but the man remained silent, like he had since their call with the JCS.

"I'm not crazy!"

"Who said you were? And remember, we live in a world where a fungus is taking over people's minds and bodies. It doesn't get crazier than that."

"I saw how Malloy looked at me. We've both seen that look. Hell, we've given that look. It's the one we save for soldiers who've snapped. But, Finn, what those infected were doing... they were communicating."

"Hey! If I thought you were crazy — if the JCS thought you had *snapped* — you wouldn't be going to New York, let alone commanding a team. And I sure as shit would have said something."

Blum pushed air from his lungs. Finn was right, understaffed or not, they wouldn't jeopardize the lives of other soldiers by putting a gun in unstable hands.

"Anyway, if I were you, I'd be more concerned about telling your mom. Chances are, she'll break your legs to keep you from deploying."

They shared a subdued laugh, but Finn wasn't wrong.

"Can I ask you a question... about your mom? Why is she..."

"Dad died a week after I got my first job. I'd just turned sixteen." Blum interrupted, he knew what Finn was asking. "Killed by some drug-addled punk robbing a house. He was a Cleveland cop. I always figured it was a combination of the things my dad told her about what he saw on the streets, and the way he died that made her the way she is. Tough as nails, with little tolerance for bullshit. Plays life close to the vest."

"That clears a lot up. She really hates Abe. What's that about?"

"You've met, Abe, right? Like I said, she can't tolerate bullshit. Perceived or otherwise."

Finn shook his head. "I don't see it. He's a pain in the ass, but the hate tossed his way seems lopsided."

"I'm pretty sure most of it started just after he moved in. Guy was nuts about his lawn, always yelling at the neighborhood kids to stay off it. Kept our baseballs if they rolled into his yard, even tried to keep one of my friend's bikes when he wiped out in those damn tier grabbers he'd edged into his lawn. I was in fourth or fifth grade at that time. My mom and him used to go rounds over the way he treated us kids."

Finn stifled his laugh. The image of Abe blistering some scared little kid was classic *mean old man*. "Meh, that shit makes me laugh. It's part of his charm."

Blum looked at Finn for the first time since leaving FOB Olmsted, a grin creeping up his cheeks. "It kinda is."

"So, we agree? Keep the whole *alive in there somewhere* INTEL to ourselves? Because, as Malloy said, alive or not, once the fungus takes hold, game's over. We can't have the community thinking about that."

Blum shook his head, still grinning. "Look at you, going battlefield shrink on me. That was crafty... but thanks for getting me outta my head. And yes, we keep it from them."

\*\*\*

Stanley scowled at the broken humanity on the roadside. Another soul lost to the ignorance of man! From behind a car's burnt husk, he'd watched the war machine intentionally strike this one hard enough to lift him from the ground and toss him like a discarded rag doll.

Had he not been delayed by avoiding the group firing their weapons wildly at the herd he'd been tracking for several miles, he could have saved this man. As it was, they'd ruined his daily collection goal, and he was lucky to escape with his life.

Seems Crystal was right about one thing. He needed a gun. Everyone had one, and he'd soon be forced to defend himself and his subjects from further persecution. An armed populace also made it nearly impossible for him to secure the sustenance his subjects required.

He could no longer dip into the well of his group to feed the souls housed in the kennels. Jenney's disappearance had changed the complexion of their relationship. But he'd only need them for a short while longer. Of that, he was certain.

***

"You want to join us for dinner at Abe's tonight? He kinda ignored my self-invitation. But we need to organize guard duties; he's not going to be happy. Should be fun."

"Hard no. I've got to tell mom what's happening. I have a three-day window to get familiar with the MOPPs and connect with my team via video before training starts at Olmsted. My plate's pretty full. Plus, if mom caught me eating dinner with Abe instead of her... all hell, Finn."

Finn had been half listening, focused instead on the vehicles they'd fallen in behind as they approached the main gate. The scavenging team was scheduled for a run, but the Humvee was not.

"Did you catch any chatter on your headset?"

Blum tapped his radio, turning it on. "My radio's been off since we arrived at Olmsted. But it's quiet, now."

Finn cursed himself. He'd also forgotten to turn his radio on. He assumed he was traveling with the only person he'd need to communicate with, but should have gone online the second they rolled out of Olmsted's gate. "Something isn't right. Other than Bobby's team, no patrols were scheduled today."

The soldiers looked at each other. "Abe!"

## Chapter 32

Finn pulled alongside the mystery Humvee. The scavenging team peeled off, en route to the supply center, which had taken over Ann's garage and parts of her basement. But it was for the Hummer he had questions.

He glanced past Blum and signaled for Randy to stop. But he pretended not to see Finn and, instead, looked into the backseat.

"Hold on!" Blum shouted as he trounced on the accelerator, cut in front of the other vehicle, grinding them to a stop.

A deep breath, meant to calm his simmering anger, failed. Finn was marching toward the Hummer the instant he killed the motor. He pointed at each of them, then to the pavement in front of him. His intent was clear.

"Squad Leader, Willings! In the briefest possible use of the English language, explain why in the actual Hell your team took an unscheduled, wholly unauthorized jaunt outside this community's gates!"

"We um, were..."

"Too long! The correct answer is, *sir, such insubordination will never be repeated*!"

"Sergeant Finn, we responded to a distress call from Bobby. With our forces otherwise occupied, or *absent*, Team Hammer deployed to offer tactical assistance to, and ensure the safe return of, the aforementioned scavenging team. Furthermore, sir, your example was neither brief nor accurate. Team Hammer awaits your apology, SIR."

Finn's eyes threatened to burst from their sockets, jettisoned by the surge of blood to his face. "Gage! Is your squad leader being truthful?"

"He is, sir."

Finn stormed back and forth, his tight marching line focused on Abe's position. How did this keep happening? How did Abe have a valid reason for his actions? And his response, sans the jab, was calm and delivered with military precision.

"Permission to speak, sir!"

Finn startled, then nodded at Abe as his pacing slowed. "Granted."

"Team Hammer acquired INTEL regarding the infected. Said INTEL is accompanied by a sample which we secured for inspection and scientific analysis, sir!"

Finn stepped nose to nose with Abe, his anger bleeding off in a trickle. "Are you feeling okay?"

"Why does everyone keep asking me that, sir?"

"No reason, just checking in. Rally at my house. We'll review your INTEL at that point." He leaned in, his mouth even with Abe's ear. "I like the call sign... It's Hammer Time!"

\*\*\*

Finn's gloved hand pushed on the Ziploc bag again. The volume had increased since he'd been inspecting it, and, according to Abe, five-fold since they'd secured what he described as an amount that would barely fill a shot glass.

"We should get this into a bigger bag. Aislan, grab two trash bags, the big ones, from the garage."

Finn set his stare on Abe and his team. "You're *sure* this is what's left of an infected?"

"We're sure," Stone answered. It seemed Finn wasn't accepting Abe's answers. "It happened to a couple of them. I can't say for certain, but I'd wager they're the same ones whose skin appeared covered with lesions."

Finn turned to Randy. "What did you see?"

Randy fidgeted. This marked the third time Finn had asked. "A puddle of that goo with clothing floating in the middle. Same as the *last* two times you asked."

"Sir, with all due respect, we should immediately transfer the sample to FOB Olmsted. I believe it's critical and presents us with, and may answer, many unknowns."

Finn stared quizzically at Abe. "You're creeping me out."

Abe exhaled as his face flushed. "Okay, which Abe do you want? I try to be more soldier-ish and I'm creepy. But, when I'm myself, I get on everybody's nerves and people want to punch me. Make up your damn minds!"

"That's better." Finn smiled. "Your team... Team Hammer, will deliver the sample to Olmsted. I'll radio them and let them know we're coming."

Finn glanced at each of them again, holding their stares for a two count. "You did good. Dismissed."

\*\*\*

"When are you going to tell them?"

Finn waited until Abe, Randy, and Stone reached the street before answering Nic. "When we get back. We'll just show up for dinner. I'm still not sure you should be there."

Nic scoffed. "I wouldn't miss it."

## Chapter 33

Thorp cringed when the discarded glass bottle shattered beneath his boot. Frozen, he strained to hear any sign that he'd given away his position. His hand brushed against the pistol stuffed in his waistband. He'd found it on their last scavenging mission. He'd never fired a gun, but having it eased his building anxiety. After all, it couldn't be that hard to operate; point it, and pull the trigger. The gun goes bang, the bad guy dies. He'd watched that exact sequence thousands of times on TV.

When nothing happened, Thorp restarted his trek. The space between the building and overgrown rosebushes was narrow. At times, so tight, he was forced to flatten his body against the building to avoid snagging his clothes on thorny branches. But he'd made it to the window. He only needed to muster the courage to look through.

The rough fabric of his shirt's sleeve cleared the moisture on his brow, but much more ran freely along his cheeks and into his scraggly beard. Thorp nearly yelped when light burst from the window, then swallowed bile rising in his throat as the yellow glow cutting through the night illuminated the ground a few yards away.

Bones, many shattered, glistened like ghoulish gemstones. He blinked away tears, but the sight still blurred. He turned his face, but found no relief, only a pile of tattered clothing. A tortured moan grew to an angry scream. Jenney's favorite belt dangled in the bushes.

A rubber coated wire strangled his scream as it tightened around his neck. His fingers dug into his skin, but the cord merely tightened the more he fought to force them under the cable. He tried to spin to his right, but was pulled left violently, then shoved into the rosebushes.

Thorp's skin laced open, his sight stolen as hundreds of thorns ripped into his face. He couldn't scream, he couldn't fight back, the coated wire had control. His hands slapped at his waistband, searching for the equalizer, his one chance to live.

The fingers on his right hand wrapped around the weapon's grip an instant before being forced into a fresh snarl of barbs. Instinct tried to pry his hand open and bring it to cover his battered face. But fear won. His grip tightened as he tore the gun from his waistband.

Thorp's arm extended behind him and he hoped it faced his unseen attacker. He pulled the trigger again and again, but nothing happened. There was no bang, no fierce recoil as the gun fired and spit out an empty shell casing. Other than his attacker pausing, the world around him hadn't changed.

His legs folded, he gasped for air, and his fate became clear when warm skin brushed against his cheek. "I told you this place was off limits. But I want you to know that I appreciate your sacrifice. My subjects crave a meal. And, although scrawny, you arrived in the nick of time. They'll be most appreciative. I'll be able to continue my work and society will honor you when I puzzle out the cure for this wretched infection."

Thorp hadn't heard most of Stanley's speech; the cable's tension had been too tight.

\*\*\*

Sampson paced the length of his otherwise empty cell and glared through its small diamond-shaped openings. The sputtering minds of the others like him had proven difficult to contact. But they knew Sampson was different. When he reached out to them, their fury would calm; they would follow him as his first soldiers had.

But The Others had to be dealt with. Caged far from Sampson and the ones like him, the do-gooder wasted food on them; food his newest soldiers needed.

\*\*\*

"I'm sorry for this one's condition. He certainly was an uncooperative dreg. However, he fulfilled one of my more urgent needs." Stanley held up Thorp's pistol as he spoke to Sampson. "I believe it may be malfunctioning. However, I'm quite the tinkerer and should have it functioning properly in no time."

Sampson's black eyes squinted at the weapon. The fighters used them to kill his soldiers. "Out," he rasped, and gave his cage door a gentile shake.

Stanley staggered backwards. "Again! Speak again!"

"Out."

Stanley's vision misted. Was this really happening? "Are you requesting to be set free from holding?"

Sampson nodded and tugged on his cage door.

"You're in there. Your mess of a brain still functions normally. I knew it was true, that I would lead you to redemption." Stanley rushed toward the cage, fumbling his keys in excited hands. "You will be their mentor — help lead them back to the light. We'll work shoulder to shoulder until we purge this blight from the earth!"

Sampson grinned when the key slid into the lock and slammed his full weight into the door the instant the bolt retracted. The impact sent Stanley stumbling backward, his arms flailed trying to recover his balance, but Sampson lashed out, sending the man cartwheeling to the polished concrete floor. Sampson loomed above the downed man, leering hungrily at his bulbous throat, then kicked the gun away.

The caged infected erupted. They pushed and struggled to get to the food. Sampson glanced at the half dozen pens holding his new soldiers.

His bare foot nudged Stanley's hand, the one still grasping the keys, and he pointed at the cages. But the do-gooder just stared with unfocused eyes. Sampson bent and grabbed a fistful of the man's thinning hair and dragged him to the nearest cage.

*\*\**

Sampson squeezed blood from his beard and licked his hand as The Others cowered to the back of their cage. He had wanted to slaughter them, but his soldiers were too few to lose even one.

They would do no harm locked away until the hunger consumed them.

# Chapter 34

Abe stood in the foyer and soaked in the stillness. It was a welcome change after his visit to FOB Olmsted. The way the CO acted when they handed over the sample and explained what had happened set his teeth to grinding.

Lieutenant Richards had summoned a hazmat crew the instant Finn pulled the Ziploc from the double-wrapped trash bags. He pummeled them with questions after the hazmat team secured the sample. Abe worried they'd done something wrong, or maybe Richards suspected them of having a hand in producing the fluff.

Then he said it; *tainted water supply*! They didn't know if the fluff had already infiltrated the supply or if water treatment chemicals would neutralize the fungus's pathogens. Or, hell, if filtering through earth would remove the contaminants.

Abe had water, hundreds of gallons stored, for just such an emergency. But his primary food supply relied heavily on clean water. "This is bullshit!"

He spun a tight circle — he was alone for the first time in weeks. He pushed away the thoughts of death by fungus-tainted water and rushed to his supply room. The secret stash, the one he'd been waiting for this very moment to dive into, beckoned him.

At the supply room door, he paused and slowed his breathing, listening for signs of Lu lurking somewhere in the house, waiting for him to let his guard down. It was silent.

The door swung open on well-oiled hinges and triggered the motion-activated lights. His crowning achievement stretched the length of the two hundred square foot room to his right. Two years' worth, at least, of freeze-dried food shared space on the floor-to-ceiling shelves with countless canned and dry goods. All sorted by expiration date, caloric content, and where they fell on his personal taste-o-meter. The back wall held his water supply. He grimaced as the day's events resurfaced.

A stroke of the cool black polymer grip of his CZ Scorpion calmed him as his eyes drifted along the collection of weapons next to it and to his left. They were his ace in the hole. And after using the mil-spec M4A1, he realized its rate of fire would deplete his ammunition supply faster than he could reload, all while killing fewer infected. He intended to use his Ruger going forward and figured Stone and Randy would do likewise.

But checking his supplies wasn't why he was here; it was the canned bacon he sought.

"Come to daddy!" he whispered while pulling ammo cans from the stack under the gun racks. He reached into the void he'd created and pulled the can marked *Special Ammo* from its hiding spot. "You are my sunshine, my only..."

"I thought I was your only sunshine?"

"Damn it! Why... how? You're rotten!" Abe slammed the ammo can back into its spot and spun to face Lu. "Why do you hate me?"

Lu chuckled. "It's empty, Abe."

"How do you know? That's my special ammo. I never used my special ammo, *Lu*!"

"Abe, Abe, *Abe*, the apocalypse hasn't magically lowered your cholesterol. You're not having a heart attack and leaving me alone to deal with this mess. Plus, you probably wouldn't die, just end up disabled, and I'd have to wheel you around for the rest of your life."

"Please, you'd wheel me outside the barrier and feed me to the first infected you found. You've been trying to kill me for years, always sneaking up on me..."

"Stop talking and grab four bags of lasagna. The good stuff, Swartz Foods."

Abe stepped deeper into the storage room, an inch out of Lu's reach. "Why? Four bags makes eight servings. Plus, it's beef lasagna. Thought you were worried about my heart?"

"Oh, never mind, I'll get it myself," Lu grumbled as she pushed past Abe.

\*\*\*

Abe stared at the deathly quiet group around his dining room table, then waved his knife in the air. "Cutting the tension. Don't mind me."

Nic startled, and began shoveling lasagna into her mouth.

"Um, babe, what'cha doing?"

"He's going to blow a gasket," Nic responded through a full mouth. "That was the first sign. I haven't had a decent meal in weeks. I'm eating as much as possible before he unhinges."

"Tell me, Nic, why would I *unhinge*? My team is here, my beautiful wife is here, and we're enjoying a delightful meal. Leading me to the assumption that you're about to lay some bullshit on me and ruin our meal."

Finn cleared his throat. "Actually, I'm the BS-layer."

"Of course you are. She's tainted you. I tried to warn you."

"Abe, here it is," Lu nearly shouted, "I'm joining the security force. With Finn deploying, the strike teams still training, and scavenging teams running regular missions, we're down headcount. So I'm joining, end of discussion."

"Me too, Randy," Bina blurted.

"Kit?" Stone asked, turning to his wife.

"Yep. Lynn will spend her days with Ann, filling in for Lu. And Aislin will work with her in the evenings, after training Team Bravo."

Abe glanced at his brother and Randy and shrugged. "Good. They're the meanest women, outside of Ann, in the community. Perfect fit."

Finn's brow arched. He turned to face Nic. A forkful of lasagna hovered an inch from her squirreled cheeks as she stared at Abe.

"However..."

"Here it comes," Finn whispered, and shut his eyes.

"I'm sorry. Would you like me to stop talking while you interrupt?" Abe continued when Finn didn't respond. "I believe, in the interest of keeping my wife, and to a larger degree, the community, safe, you should submit an equipment request for a Bradley Fighting Vehicle. During our visit to Olmsted, I noticed several unused Bradleys littering the grounds. They'd be better utilized by the citizens of this fine outpost."

*Lawyer speak*! "No. You're not getting a Bradley. The M4s and other equipment are the last you'll see for a while." Finn struggled to keep his tone flat.

"The M4s... I've decided not to use mine. Too many rounds too fast. But a BFV, now that's a force multiplier."

A pounding on the front door cut Finn's reply off. "Sergeant Finn! We need to speak. Now!"

\*\*\*

"I'm keeping mine. I've always wanted an M4. Not a chance I'm giving it up now. You know it has select-fire, right?"

"You didn't fire it, did you, Randy? We got M4A1s, not straight M4s. Tell me what you think when you're in the middle of a fight." Abe answered while watching Finn back away from Ann. He was running out of walkway and would soon step onto Abe's front yard. "If she gets him on the lawn, she's going to try to tackle him."

"I'll take that bet," Stone said as he joined Randy and Abe in the picture window. "Why's she so freaking mad?"

"Best I can tell, James is joining Finn to search for patient zero. Her shrieking is kinda muffled through the glass. Finn made the mistake of correcting her on the deployment date. She said something about three days. He said it's actually two. He hasn't gotten a word in since."

"Jay, her son's name is Jay."

"Whatever. You given any thought about the water situation?"

"Your plan with the dehumidifiers and charcoal filter is solid. We should meet with Bobby, tell him to focus on getting as many as possible. If the tests on the water supply come back positive, we've got to have a solution in place."

"Oh shit!" Randy yelled when Finn's heel edged onto grass. "She's going to take him out."

Finn glanced at the picture window with pleading eyes.

"Wave at Finn everyone." The trio's toothy grins and exaggerated waves started the same instant Finn's right foot touched down on Abe's overgrown lawn.

Ann stooped into a wrestler's stance. "Here it comes!" Randy shouted.

"Ohhh, so close," Abe exclaimed as Jay ran into the fray and scooped Ann up by her waist.

*\*\*\**

"Get out!" Lu barked while pushing Abe, Randy, Stone, and Finn over the threshold. "We'll talk about your comment later. Right now, Ann needs a minute."

Abe looked at Ann, empathy flashed through him. She looked broken as she wept uncontrollably on Bina's shoulder. It passed as quickly as it had arrived when she scowled at him and growled a muddled insult through gasping sobs. "Nasty till the end."

"Is she okay?" Blum asked from an Adirondack on Abe's porch.

"She'll calm down, but you should spend the night at my place. Let some of her rage bleed off."

"Finn, I tried to tell her, make her understand how important this is."

Abe's head tilted. Jay looked like a little kid, and he, for the first time, remembered him riding his bike around the neighborhood and chasing the little rat off his front yard.

The images replayed as they walked to Finn's, joined in his mind's eye by hundreds of other flashes of better times. This was a good neighborhood with good people and they were counting on him to keep them safe.

## Chapter 35

Kim stared at the front yard through sheer curtains, their lace pattern spun the moonlight into a thousand shapes. All of them motionless — nothing had changed in the two hours she'd been standing guard. It was still a lifeless space with children's toys strewn about.

"I've got movement." Chuck's voice, even though whispered, made her jump when it sounded over her walkie-talkie. "West — behind the fence."

Kim rushed from her position to the bedroom overlooking Chuck's guard station. The window in this room offered unobstructed views of the western approach to their small compound. It had been the perfect choice to set camp, with Lake Erie as their backyard, and a high stone wall to their east, they only had to focus on the south and west, both of which had six-foot high cyclone fences situated fifty yards from their house.

"Looks like that pack of dogs from a couple weeks ago is back," she whispered while surveying the fence line through her rifle's optics. "I see nothing on two legs, but they look like they've been feeding."

The shadowy figures, backlit by dim landscape lights, huddled at the fence's base seemed — wrong. "Chuck, notice anything?"

"No barking, little movement?"

"Hit them with your spot."

"Val gave strict orders not to use it unless we see infected."

"You willing to bet your life those things aren't an infected pack?"

Chuck's spotlight cut through the dark and bounced along the landscape as he fumbled to bring it on target.

Kim pressed the air horn button, kneeled behind the windowsill, and opened fire. "Chuck, they've already breached. Find cover," she shouted while reloading. Her first magazine had emptied too fast. She fought to reign in her emotions... but the monsters were already charging Chuck's position.

She pivoted at the sound of footfalls. Val had arrived with Ben on his heels. "What'da we got?"

"They've breached the west fence line. I'm counting a dozen infected. They're angling to isolate Chuck."

Ben bolted from the room as Val took a position next to Kim. "Shit..."

Kim didn't hear the rest of Val's statement. She'd opened fire on the leading edge of infected. They were closing fast.

Ben rocketed over the threshold and, following the muzzle flashes, cut a path for Chuck's position. Stationed on a low rise behind a pile of landscaping boulders ten yards from the house, outside guard duty was the most perilous. If the guard wasn't sharp, they'd find themselves unable to retreat.

Ben was firing as he fell in next to Chuck. His red dot bounced from target to target, but there were too many. He adjusted his aim to the breach as more appeared to sprout from the ground in front of the fence.

"Kim, Val, focus your fire at the base of the fence. They've tunneled under." He waited for a response. It came in the form of soil exploding near the fence.

"Chuck, focus right. I've got left."

Ben swept his AR across the battlefield, ending any infected bounding into his optics. But their fire seemed ineffective, merely knocking the monsters to the ground, only to watch them rejoin the charge. "Reloading," he yelled when his bolt carrier locked back. But Chuck didn't move to cover his position. His gun had gone silent.

Air whooshed from his lungs, white bolts exploded against the night sky, then blurred and twisted with his body to the ground. His legs coiled, then lashed out, striking nothing. His attacker had vanished. "Val, the door!" he screamed into his walkie.

Val listened as Ben's transmission faded to wet coughing gibberish. Kim was already moving, rushing to secure the door. Her rifle's report, steps from the door, brought him to his feet with his rifle at high ready.

The first monster through the door landed face down, inches from Val's feet, the back of its head missing, destroyed by a single round from Val's weapon. But the second and third monsters moved too fast. Their black eyes locked on their prey, they sliced through the small space before Val registered their stench. His back slammed to the hardwood floor an instant later.

He clamped his eyes shut, bracing for the pain, but they didn't bite or tear at his flesh. Instead, they pinned him to the floor. His back arched and hips twisted. This was his chance, his last opportunity to escape. He cried out as he strained against his captors, summoning the last of his strength to break free, to live.

Soil from a filthy hand splashed into his eyes, blinding him as the hand grabbed his face and forced it to still. The dirt melted his vision into a kaleidoscope of faces, all of them the same. A bearded monster, its pitch eyes glinting, pulled his face closer to its own.

Val tried to scream, but the monster's grip made it impossible. Again, he slammed his eyes shut and gagged as the stench of rotting flesh blanketed his senses.

The monster's beard scraped against his cheek, its mouth next to his ear, and pushed cool air over his jaw. Val's eyes burst open as the monster spoke. "Soldier," it rasped, before its teeth sank into his neck.

# Chapter 36

Robin lifted her head, and scanned the dock — Kim and Val should have arrived ten minutes ago. Shawn tugged her back below the boat's gunwale. "If they don't show in ten, we'll hike to the house, grab the Jeep, and double back for the fish. But I'm sure they'll show. Stop worrying."

Robin and Shawn had set sail three days ago. Their catch was mostly Lake Erie walleye and was the group's primary source of food. Val and Kim would always rally where they docked and help offload their catch, and take them home. The cycle repeated every other week, but this trip had come early. Forced on them after their freezer died and a hundred pounds of fish spoiled.

At the infection's onset, she pressed her friends to anchor off the Vermilion, Ohio, shoreline and wait it out. They rejected her idea for a host of reasons, their primary objection; being trapped thirty miles from shore when something on the boat went sideways.

Now, after she and Shawn commandeered their third boat, she understood how much could go wrong on open water. Not to mention the confined living space. Even the grandest of yachts would quickly transform into a prison with six bodies sharing a few hundred square feet.

"Do you think they forgot we switched docking locations?"

"It was Val's idea, so no, they didn't forget."

Robin stuck her head over the gunwale again and scanned the building bordering the docks. The windows of the Cleveland Yachting Club remained dark. She'd hoped to see the green glow of Val's flashlight signaling the all clear, that maybe he waited in there instead of risking the dock's open approach. She saw nothing.

"Damn it, Robin. You're going to give away our position!"

A glint of metal drew her attention to the third dock from theirs. "I think they're here, but I only see one person."

Shawn's head popped up next to Robin's. He squinted against the late dusk sky. "It's Ben! Over here," he hissed.

Ben's head jerked toward Shawn's voice. He stumbled toward the thirty-two-foot boat, rocking gently in time with the waves coming off the lake.

"Something's wrong." Robin landed on the dock, just out of Shawn's reach, the instant she stopped talking.

"Robin, get your ass back here."

She ignored Shawn and raced toward her lifelong friend. "Oh my God, Ben, what happened?"

Ben held his right hand to the side of his neck, but failed to staunch the blood flowing from a ragged wound just below his ear.

"We gotta get out of here," he gurgled. "They overran the house."

"Where're the others?"

"Robin, everyone's dead. They're all dead. I, I tried..." He trailed off as his knees failed and he slammed to the dock.

"Shawn, I need help!" Robin struggled to pull her friend to safety. Her hands kept slipping from his armpits, his weight too much for her slight frame. She grabbed his tactical vest's pull-strap and turned to drag him, but her boot shot from under her. Her knee pads clacked against the wood dock, muffled by the blood pooling from Ben's neck. "Shawn!"

Ben grabbed her calf. She could hear his wet breaths as he fought to pull himself forward. She tried to stand, to restart her effort to save him, but he'd trapped her, pinning her legs under his immense weight.

A single gunshot stung her ears an instant after Shawn had warned her to get down. She covered her head and waited for more gunfire, then spun her head wildly when it didn't come.

"He's gone. We've got to get on the lake. NOW!"

"What did you DO?" Robin sobbed as Shawn pulled her to her feet. "He was our friend!"

"He was infected and so are they." Shawn spun her to face the shambling forms rushing their position and hauled her to the boat by her belt. "He led them straight to us!"

Shawn hoisted her over the gunwale, four feet above the dock, and ran to free the forward mooring lines. He dared a glance to the infected mob — they'd halved the distance. He'd have to cut the rear lines from the boat's deck.

"Robin, I need covering fire." He questioned why she hadn't yet opened fire. "ROBIN! Shoot something!" Nothing.

As the line dropped free, Shawn drew his sidearm and sent a poorly aimed volley of 9mm rounds into the infected. Other than quickening their pace, it had little effect.

He spun and bolted for safety. They had to free the boat, they had to push off from the dock. "Damn it, Robin, do something." Shawn landed hard on the boat's deck as the infected swarmed over the mooring cleat where he'd just been standing.

On his knees, he searched for Robin. It only took a second to find her crumpled, unconscious body. The darkening lump on her forehead explained why she'd been silent — he didn't have time to determine the how — infected hands were brushing against his back.

The razor edge of his nine-inch Bowie knife severed the hands gripping the gunwale, but their sudden release rocked the craft hard to port-side. His footing followed. He was lying next to Robin before the craft tilted back to starboard, but the flash of twisted faces and black eyes spurred him to hands and knees.

A hard tug pulled Robin off the deck-mounted mooring cleat. His blade freed the line with two quick slices. "Ha, suck on that, ya freaks!"

Twelve steps was the distance Shawn had to travel to reach the helm. They'd be free of the dock in seconds. He struggled to his feet and spread his arms to steady himself against the boat's sway. He glanced starboard. The mob had grown in size and intensity, and remained close, too close. The boat should have drifted, even a short distance, from the dock immediately after he cut the line.

"No, no, no," he whispered as the dock flashed into view. The monsters had seized the forward mooring line, but that wasn't what ran ice through his veins. It was the monsters' faces. He knew them. He loved one of them. Kim was his wife. "Please, God, not her, not my Kim!"

The helm blurred as he staggered forward. He dragged a gloved hand across his eyes to clear his sight, but the helm soon blurred again.

"You sons of bitches," he growled through clenched teeth. "You're not taking me! Did you hear that?" his voice rose with each step. "You're not taking me. You'll pay for what you've done! I promise..."

His words caught in his throat, caged there by an arm gripping him from behind. Shawn slapped and pulled against the monster's filthy forearm, but couldn't break free. He thrust his body forward, trying to ruin the beast's balance. Adrenalin surged through his limbs as the monster's grip faltered. His torso twisted, his hand dropped to his waist. This was his chance.

Shawn's fingers scrabbled along his belt, searching for his blade. The monster jerked his body left, and forced his head down, then lifted him skyward. Air surged from his lungs, forced from them when his back crashed to the deck.

His head lolled to the side, leveling his eyes with his knife. It laid where he'd dropped it, next to the mooring cleat and Robin's body.

The monster kneeled at his side, its scraggly beard draped over Shawn's shoulder. "Soldier," it rasped the same instant he noticed Robin's mutilated neck.

***

Sampson crouched over the bodies, keeping his hungry soldiers at bay until his newest recruits awoke and joined his ranks. His army was growing, but it wasn't large enough, not yet. When it was, they would feed.

## Chapter 37

Abe took care to avoid walking in front of Ann's house, instead cutting across lawns on his side of the street en route to Finn's. She'd kept a low profile since Jay had broken the news two days ago. But Lu had warned him to keep his tender parts outside of her arm's length. Apparently, she blamed every man in the community for her son's choice.

He switched the plastic shopping bag to his left hand, and rested his right on his sidearm when he saw her round the corner a hundred yards ahead, and silently thanked God he'd missed her when she set out.

As he neared the corner, he noticed many of his neighbors heading in the same direction. All of them with the same intent; to say goodbye and wish their friends good luck.

"Still bullshit," Abe grumbled. "They abandoned you. We're your family now. You should tell them to f..."

"Who ya talking to?"

"For the last time, stop sneaking up on me." Abe's teeth gritted, but he took Lu's hand in his.

She didn't object to his tight grip. She knew her husband. He was sad and being sad made him angry. Over the years, she'd taken to referring to it as sangry. "He's going to be okay. Finn's a soldier, and he's tough as nails. He'll be home lickety-split."

"They abandoned him, Lu — left him to die. Now, they're sending him to some hellhole. It's not right!"

Lu tugged Abe to a stop and cradled his face in her hands. "That's not for you to decide, it's Finn's choice. He's fighting because that's what soldiers do. They fight to keep us safe. And right now, he needs you to be strong so he can focus on his mission. Show him his family's safe with you at the helm."

"Yeah, but..."

"But nothing, Abe. We're going to wish him well, and that's *all* we're going to do. He's made his decision. He will leave our gate knowing we're safe."

Abe nodded and took Lu in his arms. He wasn't as confident as her, but he'd die trying.

\*\*\*

The festive atmosphere swirling around the soldiers took Abe aback. It jolted his anger at first, but he replayed Lu's words, and stuffed his emotions. This wasn't about anything other than their friends, the soldiers that had kept them safe.

"Okay, I'm good." He let go of Lu's hand. "Go have some fun. We've earned it."

He wandered through the strangers, many of whom stopped to greet or thank him.

"Do you know any of them?"

"Not a soul, Randy."

He glanced at his friend and smiled. "But it doesn't matter, does it? We're still Team Hammer and we're looking for a nail to drive!"

Randy chuckled and shoved a forkful of chili-covered noodles into his mouth. "Where'd you get that? I'm starving."

"Nic brought it. She set up a table next to the wives."

"Nic brought it? From where?" Abe stiffened, then searched his key ring. His head slumped. The storage room key was missing. "Looks good," he said, forcing a smile and screaming Lu's words in his head. "Think I'll get me some. Need another helping?"

"I'm good. But before you go — did you hear that firefight last night?"

"There's gunfire every night, but nothing stood out."

"This wasn't the norm. Someone was putting up a hell of a fight. It was north of us. Near the lake, best I could tell. We should probably check it out."

"Alright, we'll roll on it tomorrow. But right now, I need to eat."

*\*\**

"When you get back, we'll get to work securing a Bradley," Abe said after Finn broke from hugging Nic. "And you should bring Thor back, a dog needs a yard to play in."

Finn smiled. "Sure thing."

The men stood quietly before Abe cleared his throat. "You, ah, take care of yourself, Finn. We have a lot to do when you get home."

Finn wrapped his friend in his arms and was surprised by the strength in Abe's embrace. "I'll keep them safe, Finn. I promise," Abe whispered. "You go do what you have to do, and don't worry about us. I'll keep them safe. We'll keep a light on for you."

"Thank you, my friend," Finn whispered back before breaking their embrace. "I've got to say goodbye to Aislin."

"Who?" Abe laughed at Finn's distress. "Gotcha."

He left his friend to say his goodbyes and untied the plastic shopping bag from his belt loop as he walked toward Blum.

"Jay, this is for you. Sorry about your balls... your, your baseballs." Abe shoved the bag into Blum's hand and clamped his mouth.

"No shit!" Blum mumbled as he stared into the bag.

"I counted twenty-one. Thought if you get some down time, you may want to toss them around."

"Thanks, Abe. That sounds nice."

Abe nodded and turned. "Take care of yourself. I'll keep an eye on your mom while you're gone," he said over his shoulder as he walked away.

\*\*\*

In the Hummer's backseat, Finn watched Blum rummage through a plastic bag. He'd grab something, look at it for a minute, smile, and repeat.

"What's in the bag?"

"You might be right about Abe. He's a good dude," Blum answered as he handed Finn a dirty baseball.

Finn smiled as he read the message. *When you get home, Nic is moving in with you. Stay frosty. We need you.*

"He had people from the neighborhood write messages. There's a couple for each of us."

Finn nodded and stuffed the ball into a cargo pocket. Staying frosty was the only promise he could keep.

## Chapter 38

Abe sat quietly; his decision anxiously awaited by Team Hammer. "You're sure it was out of the north?"

"That's the only thing I'm sure of. It wasn't loud enough to be closer than four miles away," Randy answered.

"We're burning fuel, brother."

"I know, Stone. But we'll burn more wandering along the lakeshore searching for signs of a firefight. Did you talk to Bobby? Has his crew worked to our north?"

"Negative on both. But this is a good opportunity to scout the area. Make sure it's safe for his team to scavenge."

"Solid point. Randy, go north on Dove and left on Lakeshore. I'm guessing whoever it was used the lake as a natural barrier."

Randy tapped the accelerator, then stood on the brake. "Did you see that?"

"Hammer Actual, this is Hammer Four." Gage's voice was crystal clear in their headsets as he hailed them from the trailing Humvee. "Movement fifty yards to the northwest, under the curbside pine trees."

*I wish we still had Ma Duce.* "Roger, Hammer Four. Randy identified same. Northwest tower, have you detected any movement to our northwest?"

"Negative. Identify the location you want me to focus on."

After identifying the target location, Abe waited for the tower to respond, while chewing on his next move. "Abe, I have no movement, but there's some brightly colored fabric that wasn't there this morning. Do you want me to send a warning shot?"

"Tower, send one shot twenty feet up the tr..."

A pink flash, scrambling from cover cut Abe off.

\*\*\*

"Don't shoot!" *Please, don't let them shoot me.* "I'm unarmed." *Filthy and hungry, but unarmed.* "I'm petitioning for safe refuge and request to be unharmed until such petition has been adjudicated."

\*\*\*

Abe shook his head, the frazzled woman looked familiar, her pseudo-intellectual speech had removed all doubt.

"*Unharmed until such petition has been adjudicated.* Who talks like that?"

"Randy, that's none other than Stanley's wife, Cathy."

"Crystal, Abe. Stanley's wife's name is Crystal."

"Whatever, Stone. I'm busy weighing the implications of running her over. Stanley has to be close. If we kill her, he probably won't try to get back into the community."

Abe looked around the Humvee. His team was staring at him with varying degrees of shock etched on their faces. "What? Do you really want to let the dumbass rejoin our community?"

"I'm alone," Crystal yelled, as if responding to Abe. "I possess information regarding my husband. Information of upmost importance."

"Hammer Actual for Hammer Five. You're up." Abe had taken care to team Nic with Gage in the support Humvee.

"Why me, Abe? Because I'm a woman? I say we run her over."

Abe nodded. "I agree. But the bleeding hearts want to take her into custody."

He looked at Stone and Randy, neither appeared to be in a rush to approach the woman.

"I'm begging you to show mercy. Please refrain from placing the burden of Stanley's transgression at the feet of his innocent wife." Crystal fell to her knees and raised her arms high above her head and began sobbing.

"For shit's sake, she's going to bring a colony of infected to our doorstep." Abe pushed open his door as he spoke, and locked Randy in a hard stare. "She so much as flinches, shoot her."

\*\*\*

"How many?"

"I've told you three times, Abel."

"Tell me again!"

Crystal recoiled against Abe's sharp tone. "At least a dozen. But I left over a week ago, so there may be more. He calls them his subjects. Thinks he can cure them."

Abe glared at the woman; her grimy face and filthy clothing lined up with her story. But trusting her was impossible. "I'm telling you, if Randy and Stone report that the house isn't exactly as you described it, we're putting you out!"

His headset filled with static before Randy's voice faded in. "Abe, her story checks out. Judging by the empty cans, she lived here a week plus. Found a knife, empty backpack, and binoculars in the upstairs bedroom. She was definitely watching us."

Abe stiffened and turned back to Crystal. "Misty Meadows Boarding and Kennels?"

Crystal nodded.

"Randy, we'll be waiting for you at the gate."

## Chapter 39

It would have been their third slow pass of the property when Abe called a halt, prompting Randy to pull their Humvee to a stop on the apron of their target location. The hand-drawn map, as best he could tell, was perfect.

"Listen up. Carrie's map looks pretty accurate. She indicated the infected are being held in the outbuilding twenty yards from the main structure. We can expect, at her last count, between ten to twelve uninfected residents and a dozen plus infected. Stanley refused to allow them to arm themselves with more than bludgeoning weapons. However, if they attack, shoot."

"Who's Carrie? I thought this was Crystal and Stanley's place?"

Abe ignored Randy and pushed forward. "We're *not* getting pulled into another trap. Gage, Nic, I want you on the main structure's east and west flanks, just inside the tree line, with the fence at your backs. Anything creeps from the house, tree line, or street, shoot it. Stone's on the outbuilding's rear approach. He's going to be out of your sightlines, so stay tight on your coms. Randy and I will breach the main structure first, clear it, then breach the outbuilding."

Abe waited for his team to confirm. When they finished, he added, "We're in and out in fifteen. Let's roll."

Team Hammer, despite their full battle rattle, moved silently into position. The mid-day sun punched through the surrounding oak trees' canopy in brilliant shafts, while large swaths of the property remained dusky. If a target sprinted through the grounds, the strobing effect would make it difficult to identify the target as infected. Abe was sure innocent blood would spill and prayed it wouldn't be theirs.

"On three," Abe whispered.

"On three," Randy confirmed as he leaned forward, turned the doorknob, and pushed the door open. "Finn told me to work on my breaching," he responded to Abe's baffled stare.

"Looks like someone's not getting their security deposit back," Abe whispered as they entered the living room, his comment in response to the room's chaotic state. "Shit! Eyes wide, we have blood."

"Abe," Stone's voice rattled Abe's headset, "it looks like a civil war hospital back here. I've got arms and legs everywhere. Crystal wasn't bullshitting."

"Stone, can you get elevated?"

"Negative. But I'm in a solid defensive position. Just roll your ass."

Abe glanced at Randy, and nodded. "Is anyone here? We mean you no harm!"

They waited a five count, straining to hear a response to Abe's shouted message. "Okay, they know we're here. Let's blitz it. Stay three paces back."

Abe and Randy tore through the house and found devastation in every inch. Whoever had been here had waged a vicious war.

"Abe, why no bodies or body parts? With the amount of blood we're finding, we should have stumbled across a carcass by now, especially if they were attacked by infected."

"Stone!" Abe yelled as understanding washed over him. "Get your ass outta there. Link up with Nic. We're exiting now."

Abe was running the instant Stone radioed his confirmation.

\*\*\*

The team stacked up to the left of the kennel's entrance. Abe wasn't taking any chances. The infected were loose; he was sending the entire team. He and Randy would breach; Stone, Nic, and Gage would follow twenty seconds later. They would shoot on sight.

"On three."

"On three," Randy confirmed and slammed his foot onto the door.

Shards of wood pelted Abe as he moved on contact and slid to a stop four steps into the gloom. "Hold!"

Randy stumbled to a stop next to him and followed the beam of Abe's weapon-mounted light. "What the..."

"Talk to us, Abe!"

"Gage, this place is full of broken dreams, bad smells, and leftovers. Nic, Gage, cover the door. Stone, rally up."

The trio inched through the murk — their weapon lights flashing across one gruesome scene after another.

"What the hell was he doing?" Abe wondered aloud as his light traveled the length of a metal gurney, the type used in every morgue scene Hollywood produced over the last thirty years. But this one sported thick leather straps stewing in a puddle of bodily fluids.

"SITREP."

Abe jolted when Gage's voice pierced through his headset. "If one more person does that to me, I swear to sweet baby Je..."

A thud and strangled rasp cut Abe off, and pulled his attention to the back of the kennel. He noticed, for the first time, dozens of cages lined the kennel's walls. The closest sat with their gates ajar, interiors heavy with debris, but mercifully empty.

"This is a joke, right? A sick joke."

"Whatcha got, Randy?"

Light bursting from the ceiling forced Abe to squint against its harsh florescent glare. His sight adjusted and Randy's hulking frame came into view, his hand still grasping the pull chain for the bank of lights he'd found.

"Heads up would've been nice, jacka..."

Abe's rant faded as his mind raced to piece together the scene mere feet beyond his friend, where Stanley, only his head visible above a dog-grooming table, sat watch over a cage packed tight with infected. The man's eyes fluttered open; they were tar black. He tried to sit forward, to stand, but only his head moved. It rocked forward again, then slammed against the chair's headrest.

Abe trailed Stone as they rushed to support their friend — he'd frozen and would make for easy prey.

"Whoa!" Abe yelled as he twisted to a stop at Randy's side. What he saw explained Randy's absence of fear when facing an unrestrained monster. And thumped a reality into his chest that stole years from his life — these things had sent a message — no living being was safe.

Stanley's head sagged heavily, so much so his chin should have touched his flabby chest; instead, it rested against the glistening bones protecting his empty chest cavity. They had stripped his body clean.

"I'll never sleep again," Stone muttered.

Fluff oozed along Stanley's cervical vertebrae and pushed Randy past reason and self-control. He ended the monster with a single defining gunshot.

***

Gage kneeled and swept his hand through the grass, then rubbed his fingers together. "They traveled toward the back of the property. Single file. It's been a while since they passed." He pointed at a stack of cut wood piled against the iron fence. "And that's their egress point."

Abe moved closer to the former infantry man. The air grew cooler as he put several yards between his body and the kennel's smoldering flames.

"Can you track them?"

"Sure, to a point. I'm looking at about three acres of woodland before I reach the closest subdivision — Lakeview. It's gated.

Ninety percent of those houses skirt Erie. Gives them a lot of places to hide and target our approach."

"I'll go with you. The team can follow on surface streets."

"Abe, did you hear what he said?"

"Yes, *Randy*. I heard what he said. Did you hear what *I* said?"

"Yes, *Abe*. I heard what you said. That's why I asked, because you may have heard him, but ya sure as hell weren't listening."

"I WAS. He said we have three or four acres until we hit the... lakeshore. Got it. Try being a little clearer, Randy. We wasted valuable time working through your puzzle."

"Timeout! Don't you find it odd they left some of their own behind? I'm almost onboard with your flimsy theory about why they stripped Stanley clean. But the more bodies they have, the more food they find. Right? So why leave hunters behind?"

"Nic, do you need me to talk slower? I can, if it'll keep you up to speed?"

Nic's head tilted, her eyes merely dark slits. "You said nothing about the infected left behind."

"Sure I did. Randy, please bring *Nasty* Nic up to speed while I devise a superior strategy."

"Actually, I was waiting for your explanation."

*Did I hallucinate the conversation about the warring factions?* "The opposing variants? What Blum told us about them fighting? Ring a bell?"

"Yeah, we remember. Try connecting the dots. Make it relevant to what we saw," Stone said evenly.

"The ones left behind are competition — the enemy. Get your heads in the game, people. I can't spell everything out for you!"

"*Now* it's relevant," Stone mumbled.

"Plus, this," Abe swept his hand toward the fence, "is what we were leaving to investigate before Cynthia showed up. What Randy puzzled through is what that firefight he heard means. This group, the one that got away, found food and the food fought back."

"They've also got about a thirty-six-hour head start," Gage interjected. "Picking up their trail outside of the woods is unlikely."

Abe glanced at each member of his team. Gage was right; they'd burn gallons of fuel on a fruitless search. But the lives of the living, even though strangers, could depend on his decision. Their set jaws and hard stares told him what he already knew.

"We make one pass through Lakeview."

## Chapter 40

Brenda covered her mouth, stifling her scream, and endured the tickle of blood as it traced her cheek and gurgled into her ear. The floorboards, mere inches from her face, rattled again with a deep resonating thud, wafting more crimson particulate onto her face.

She wanted to turn her head, to face her husband laying at her side, but she was paralyzed by the shadows ravaging their friends. What if they detected her movement through the small gaps in the floorboards? They'd rip through them in seconds and consume her just as quickly. Her eyes closed tight and her body trembled at the thought.

Situated at the bottom of the beach's bluff and connected to the main home's property by a single steep, winding staircase, the boathouse had seemed a perfect place to hide from the cannibalistic savages. It was old, but its roughhewn frame and rugged construction had been updated with high-end modern conveniences. It had proven more comfortable than the home they'd lived in for the better part of five years, and would easily endure the often tumultuous Northeast Ohio weather.

She'd loved the floors, original to the structure, their wide planks sanded smooth, but the owners took care to leave the flaws and variations untouched. Now trapped in the tiny space created by the raised foundation, she cursed them for not filling the gaps; the same gaps which allowed the essence of the families they shared the home with to run freely onto her face.

"We have to get to the boat." Chris' voice in her ear, barely above a whisper, jolted her. What he said filled her mouth with nausea.

She shook her head in tiny, rapid strokes. The trek to the boat garage was impossible with the monsters feasting above them. They'd be forced to inch their way twenty feet to the foundation's edge and kick through the home's skirting into the garage. And, barring their capture and death before they accomplished that nearly impossible task, the boat sat three feet above the water's surface on its hydraulic lift. They'd be swarmed long before the boat's hull sank into the lake's murky water.

"We have to. I'll be right next to you. I promise."

Chris grabbed her hand, steadying it with his fierce grip. "Stay on your back, as flat as possible." A thunderous crash silenced him for a moment. "Push with your feet and hands. Slow and steady."

Brenda flinched with each scrape of her shoulder blades along the unfinished concrete. The sides of her legs were slick with viscous moisture. She knew what the liquid was, but shoved the image from her mind.

She should have heeded Chris' warning and worn jeans and a long-sleeved shirt. But the growing summer heat, and false sense of security, led her to scoff at the suggestion. Her shorts and tank top, proper attire for collecting fishing bait, were now proving woefully inadequate for escaping the infected.

"Just a few more feet." Chris' whisper sounded as if he'd screamed, and she understood why. The chaos above them had settled as the infected fed — her friends were dead, their struggle terminated by the monster's brutal feast.

She nodded her understanding and, unable to tolerate the slow rolling moisture, brought a hand to her brow. Brenda's head shook, her neck arched, as her eyes filled with the concrete dust coating her hands. It ripped into her eyes with the ruthlessness of glass shards. Tears flooded her sight, but the debris only thickened.

Her body shuddered as liquid splashed over her turned face. She forced her eyes open and sighed heavily. She'd expected a red hue to fill her vision. Instead, she found Chris. His small canteen held an inch above her face, pouring the last of his water into her stinging eyes.

"Shake your head. That's all I can do for you until we're on the boat."

With her head still turned, she blinked furiously, and did as he instructed, clearing enough rubble to see the shafts of light filtering from the floor above.

"Ready?" he asked as he retook her hand in his.

She nodded and rolled her head to face the floor above. Her hope surged — she recognized where they were. She could tell by the large hollow knot in the floor. The edge of the house was only three feet away, their impossible trek had taken an hour but was nearing its end.

She flinched against the thud. Her mind spiraled as the image cleared. The single ice-blue eye staring at her was unmistakable. Shelly was dead. A memory flashed to the woman's terrified face as she ran from the beach, screaming her warning of the approaching infected. Without her selfless act, Brenda and Chris wouldn't have had time to escape through the crawlspace access panel. They'd held it open as long as they could, pleading with their friends to join them, but they refused. Instead, they took up their feeble weapons in an ill-fated attempt to defend their home. Their bravado crumbled as the first infected crashed through the patio door, steps behind Shelly.

Brenda shrieked when a black orb appeared in the void, displacing the ice-blue eye with a ruthless shove. Chris didn't know what had happened, only that his wife had rolled to her belly and raced away on elbows and knees — the skin scoured off her back as it battered along the floorboards.

"Brenda! Slow dow..." Chris froze as two fingers plunged through a gap in the floor. The insanity above them revived as the fingers curled over the plank and pulled.

Steps echoed through the crawlspace as countless infected searched for another opening, while others pounded on the aged hickory trying to get to the food beneath.

A sharp crack at the far end of the space broke Chris' stupor and sent him army-crawling after his wife. A cautious glance over his shoulder pushed him forward — an infected was peering through a jagged hole, its black eyes probing the dimly lit space for its next meal.

"Move, Brenda, move!"

Light strobed in front of him, then nearly blinded him as it burst through a jagged opening. His wife's shadow plunged him into darkness as she wiggled through and turned to face him. "FASTER, Chris, they're right behind you!"

She latched onto his hands as they slapped at the skirting. She struggled to her feet and pulled. Her bowed back screamed as fiercely as her legs. But it was working — he was free to his waist and kicking frantically to push the rest of his body into the garage.

"Start lowering the boat. I've got it from here."

She didn't argue and dropped his hands. He looked at her, his eyes wide, his mouth warped in a silent scream, before he disappeared.

"Noooo!" she pleaded through gritted teeth, dropped to her knees, and reached into the shadowy opening. A hand latched onto hers. She tensed, ready for infected teeth to sink into her flesh, but another hand tugged on her arm.

"Pull!" And she did. Her will galvanized by fear and anger, her lean muscular frame surged backward, pulling Chris free. The sudden movement wrenched his legs from infected hands. He spun to his back and slammed his boot into the monster whose grasp he'd escaped. "Lower the boat!"

Brenda had been moving the instant Chris slid free. She knew the lift needed thirty seconds to lower the boat into the water. She feared they had far less time.

An eternity passed as she listened to the hydraulics hiss under pressure and watched Chris hold the infected at bay.

"Now!" she screamed as water rippled under the boat and she leapt to its deck. The powerful motor lowered and revved as Chris tumbled over the gunwale and spun. The infected was mid-flight when the boat's hull rose from the water, pushed by the 200 horsepower Mercury, an instant before it crashed into the clear fiberglass door they'd failed to open.

# Chapter 41

Lieutenant Richards watched the video feed jostle as the cameras, mounted to the team's hazmat suits neared the lump of gray fluff. He sat forward when the feed stabilized.

"What am I looking at?"

"Lieutenant, that's a fruiting body, the darkly pigmented stroma, or stalk." Doctor Lila Abram's gloved hand entered the video holding a long pointer and drew his attention to the focus of her discovery. "The spherical structure it supports is the perithecia. And its presence is possibly the single most devastating development in our already apocalyptic scenario."

"Explain."

"Lieutenant, the perithecia is the fungus' spore-bearing sexual structure. When it ruptures, the spores within will be deposited as far and wide as the breeze transporting them dictates."

Richards recoiled. The magnitude of the infection's potential spread just reached extinction level. "How do we contain it?"

"Along with a soil sample, I'm going to collect a specimen perithecia to study. I request you contact General Malloy and instruct him to secure as many DARPA resources as possible."

The Lieutenant glanced at his admin. The young man was accessing their secured network before Richards addressed Abram. "Doctor, you said *one of?*"

The doctor answered by sweeping her camera across the area. "What I'm seeing is quite remarkable."

Richards leaned to within inches of the monitor. The scene appeared as Abe, in his unstable rant, described it — scattered with dead infected. It was actually quite unremarkable, until the camera focused on a mound of fluff and followed a network of tendrils, emerging from its side, along the overgrown lawn, where they terminated into a second mound.

The camera panned the length of the yard. There were seven such mounds, each with perithecia sprouting two feet skyward from center mass.

"I'll be securing a section of the tendrils as well. Then, I believe we should incinerate the remaining examples. We'll place containment bags over their perithecia to interrupt spore release until your team's weapons are deployed. I now appreciate your insistence on including the thermobaric weapons with our security detail."

Richards, against the doctor's wishes, had risked equipping two members of the doctor's detail with XM1060 — 40mm grenades. The ordnance would be delivered via picatinny rail-mounted M203 grenade launchers. He speculated the 1060s combined overpressure and extreme heat would expand the initial kill radius, while the resulting fireball drove away combatants unaffected by the primary blast. They were only a stopgap until the military could locate sufficient numbers of mothballed M9-7 flamethrowers.

"This isn't the purpose I had in mind when I assigned them. Exercise extreme caution while those ordnances are deployed, Doctor. Actually, I prefer you're well clear of the area prior to discharge."

"I will, for reasons of scientific observation, retreat with your men to the required minimum safe distance."

"Of course, Doctor. But please remember, we can't afford to lose you."

Richards watched the Doctor's team secure large, bright red, bio containment bags over multiple perithecia. The image blurred momentarily when the doctor turned to supervise her team's harvesting of the study specimen.

The revolting growth appeared to twitch as they lowered the containment bag over it, but they sealed the bag before he could give it a second thought. Her team then slid it into a large, wheeled drum and secured the lid.

\*\*\*

Richards watched the heat waves pulse across the lawn as his soldiers walked their fire through the target zone rapidly. He'd expected thermal lift to carry the containment bags from the fluff mounds, but was pleased to see them constrict, and burst into flames.

His risk had paid off. He and Doctor Abram had just developed a new set of ROEs. Ones that could save millions of lives.

# Chapter 42

"Hoochie mama, these people were loaded!" Abe mumbled as they passed a home the size of a city block. "Can you imagine the toys they had? No wonder they gated themselves off."

"Gage for Abe, we've finished our sweep. No signs of our target. En route to our rally point."

"Shooting blanks on this side as well. See you in four."

"Is that why you never had kids?"

Abe's features pinched and his head snapped to face Randy. "What the hell are you talking about? See, this is what I meant when I said you all need to get your heads in the game. Why in the actual hell you thought to ask such a personal, and idiotic, question while we're hunting savages in the streets... I don't know — it boggles the mind!"

"So, you're not sterile?"

"No, Randy. Damn it, man, focus!"

"Then why'd you tell Gage you were sterile?"

Abe rubbed his temples, then dragged his hand down his face. "I'm not sure why I try. All day, every day, I'm working to keep everyone safe. And this, this *crap* is my thanks! At no point did I tell Gage I'm sterile."

"I'm with Randy." Stone leaned forward, filling the gap between the front seats. "You told Gage you were shooting blanks."

"Shooting blanks means *not finding*, or *fruitless search*, and can also mean *no luck*."

"Nope, it means *no swimmers*, or *impaired swimmers*, and can also mean *impotent*. Are you impotent, Abe?"

"Another reason... Lu should have never... married you!" Nic's slight came in short bursts, bracketed by snorting laughter.

"What's that? Randy, back up. Between the Tudor and contemporary."

"The *what*?"

"The brick house with fake wood beams and the glass monstrosity next to it."

"What'd you see?" Abe asked above the whine of the transmission traveling too fast in reverse.

"On the lake, looked like... it is! Someone's on the jetty, waving a flag. About ten yards from the break wall." Stone pointed toward the area. "Randy, can you get us closer?"

The trio rushed to the bluff's edge, twenty feet from where they'd been forced to leave the Humvee. Gage roared to a stop an instant later.

"She's in trouble." The woman, waving what looked like a brightly colored life vest, seemed to hear Stone's assessment. She jumped and waved frantically, then pointed forcefully east.

"Well, we found 'em." Abe searched the beach, looking for more survivors. Except for the innumerable infected, he found only sand. "They're after her."

His hand rose above his head, flattened, signaling his team to kneel. "I don't think they've seen us. We have to cut them off, or at least redirect them. Stone, what's your best guess on distance?"

Stone rose to a stoop. "Crow flies — one hundred fifty yards from here to the beach. Forty-three yards to the shoreline. Infected are a hundred seventeen yards from the jetty, give or take. We've got beach access stairs, west, twenty-three feet. We're twelve feet above the beach."

Abe chewed on Stone's curiously detailed information. Moving targets at a hundred plus yards were hittable, but they'd burn a lot of ammunition and have little to show for their efforts.

"Gage, Nic, follow the bluff east seventy-five yards and find cover. Ensure you have clear sight lines to the beach. On my order, fire on the infected. Slow — five count between each round."

"Abe, we're running out of time." Stone edged forward, his boots cresting the bluff's rim.

"Gage, Nic, one more thing. I'm not impotent, poor choice of words. GO!"

"You going to share?"

"Randy, I'll share when my strategy gels. Right now, the best I've got is Gage and Nic creating a diversion."

"Is that what we're calling it now? Or, are you saving the *engage* part for me?"

"Eh, tomato tomahto."

"The lady's running out of time, Abe. What's the plan?" Stone had risen to near-standing and his hands pulsed on his rifle.

"Alright, when I give the order for Nic and Gage to open fire, we count to ten and hit the stairs. Stone, you hold at the halfway point. Pick off any infected that don't take the bait. Randy, you're on my six. You'll hold on the beach at the end of the jetty. I'll retrieve the target. Check her for infection, and roll back to shore. Easy peasy."

\*\*\*

Stone peeled off and set up a firing position on the bluff's scraggy face, concealed by tall beach grass and positioned perfectly to intercept stray infected.

Abe's foot hit the coarse Lake Erie sand ten seconds later, and he dug his boots in for the charge.

"Abe, your tomato tomahto comment — you used it wrong. Engaging and distraction... wicked different things."

"*Randy*, focus! We've got a job to do."

The gunfire from above had pulled the infected off course. They wandered along the bluff's base, craning their necks and sniffing for the source. The volleys hadn't devastated their ranks, only downed the pack's slowest members, but that wasn't the goal. Abe and Randy needed time. It was working.

Abe spun when a third gun opened up. Stone's voice was in his ear a second later. "They've lost interest. Heading your way!"

Abe glanced to his left. The wall of death was marching directly at them.

Randy's feet slid until he regained control, but Abe didn't let him go, and dragged him toward their target. Caught too far from the stairs, the jetty was their only option. "We'll set up at fifteen feet. If they give chase, they'll bottleneck and we open up," he said as he released his grip. "Stone, Nic, Gage. Mop them up from behind. Watch your lines of fire. Shooting your team lead takes points off your score. I'm talking to you, Nic."

The infected struggled forward, slowed by the uneven and shifting sand, but didn't stop. They'd focused on the food. They wanted the food!

The frantic woman didn't move when they trundled onto the stone jetty, remaining at least ten yards away. Abe saw no weapons, or any that would have a meaningful impact on their fight. She was yelling, but the lapping water, gunfire, and his labored breathing drowned her words. He held up a palm and prayed she knew its meaning. If she approached, while he and Randy focused on the monster rushing the mouth of the jetty, and without checking her for bites, he'd be forced to end her. He took in her bright red shirt and signaled her to get down. She responded by lying flat, disappearing behind a lump of rags he hadn't noticed.

"Something's happening!"

Abe heard his brother's voice, but couldn't ask him for clarification. The infected had reached the jetty's mouth. He went to a knee and leveled his optics hip-high.

"Randy, hold fire. We want them packed tight," Abe whispered. The throng surged as one, consuming the gap between them like a pack of wolves, their focus unwavering, their hunger unending.

"Now!"

## The Wild Ones

Randy's M4 blistered the leading infected which had broken from the pack with unparalleled speed. Abe shifted to the trailing monsters, his aim low, legs crumbled under his salvo.

"That was a lot of rounds!"

"Switch to *semi-auto, Randy*."

"Now's not the time for I told ya so!" Randy clicked the rifle's fire selector to semi-auto, and opened up.

"Their main force is pulling back, retreating the way they came," Stone's incredulous tone matched Abe's reaction. *They never abandon an easy meal.*

"Anyone have eyes on the cause?" Abe adjusted his aim left, downing a straggler.

"I've got eyes on a couple of structures," Gage answered. "I see no movement inside or near either."

"Randy — covering fire." Abe stood, dropped back two feet, swung his rifle east, and focused on the herd. The scene through his optics made one thing clear; *something* was leading them.

His AR bounced on its single point sling as he swapped it for binoculars and focused on the retreating infected. A tall, wiry man, naked from his waist up, pushed and shoved against a faction still pressing forward. The herd swallowed him an instant later.

"Randy, this is starting to feel *Resident Evil*-ish."

"Reloading."

Abe spun toward his kneeling friend. The last infected was bearing down on him. He brought his rifle up, but merely held his binoculars at high ready. The monster launched himself at Randy.

Abe's eyes widened; he wouldn't bring his weapon on line in time to save his friend. He hurled the binoculars at the infected, his body followed, and spun sideways as his foot clipped Randy's shoulder. The monster had committed and matched Abe's passion to reach Randy.

The grind of bone ended with a sharp snap. Abe's clothesline blow leveled the pathetic beast on the downside of its arching attack.

"Jesus! Abe, I nearly shot you!" Randy ignored the crippled monster's undulating mouth as he rushed to his friend's side.

Abe remained facedown and motionless. "I think I hurt myself. Can't move my arm, side's on fire. Did I get him? I'm hurt. Can't breathe."

Randy tugged on Abe's vest, searching for wounds.

"Are you trying to kill me, Randy? I told you I'm hurt because I'm *actually hurt*. STOP touching me."

Randy waved to the team, a silent but urgent call for help, then spun to his feet and began a heel-toe trek toward the woman still huddled behind a mound of tattered rags.

His rifle stayed tight to his shoulder as he closed to within two feet. "Are you bitten or scratched?"

The woman's head rose above the rags... rags that rustled strangely in the light breeze. "No, but my husband needs a doctor."

Randy, on instinct, stepped back. The lump of rags was alive. "We've got two. One has a head wound. I need help inspecting them for bites."

Nic pulled up next to Randy, her head tilted. The woman's red shirt was cracked and peeling around her shoulders and elbows. Light red fabric, similar to spaghetti straps, appeared to rest on top of the shirt. "Oh shit! She's covered in blood."

Randy's finger tensed on his trigger. "No, please, we're not infected. Our boat sank," she pointed to the shallow water surrounding them. "We had to crawl under... please don't kill us." The woman's words faded under heavy sobs. She gripped her husband's clothing and buried her face.

Randy kept his rifle trained on the couple and glanced to the murky water. "She's not lying. I've got a boat hull just under the surface. What's the call, Nic?"

Nic edged forward. "Stand up, raise your hands over your head, and turn."

Randy kneeled next to the man as Nic tried to inspect the woman's gore-covered body. "What's your name?"

The man's eyes fluttered. He was swaying in and out of consciousness.

"Chris," he answered, his voice shallow and dry.

Randy rolled Chris from side to side. His neck and face, save the large gash on his forehead, were clear of bite marks or scratches. "He looks clean. Yours?"

"I can't tell if she's bitten, but her body looks like someone beat her with a belt sander. Lady, dip yourself in the water and rinse. Get as clean as possible."

"Stone, Gage, we've got a situation. Is the area clear? Is Abe mobile?"

"Area is clear, but we shouldn't grow roots. Abe is on his feet gimping around like an old man, crotchety like one, too. Helluva bruise on his side, things look broken."

"Gage, do you have zip ties? We can't give them a thorough inspection, not quick enough, anyway. We need to restrain them until we can."

"Oh my God! What happened to you?" Nic's statement pulled Randy's attention. Water ran in red rivulets over skin glistening with friction burns. As Randy stared, the intensity of the burns became clear. Most of her back and large swaths of her arms and legs were ravaged.

"Gage, we're going to need bandages. Lots of bandages."

***

From behind the beach grass' tall, gently swaying reeds, Sampson's soldiers darted through his vision on hands and knees, exposing the fighters between flashes of tattered rags and ravaged flesh. The fighters had tricked them, attacking from many places, and claimed too many of his soldiers.

They had fed in the house only a short while earlier. He would force them to wait for their next meal. Sampson had saved them from themselves, from their hunger, their sputtering minds. He needed them. He needed more of them. The building full of food awaited their arrival.

## The Wild Ones

Sampson's neck arched, thrusting his face into the breeze; the air carried the fighter's scent — he would remember this fragrance.

# Chapter 43

Abe fumed quietly. He'd been waiting hours for Jerry or Lydia to pay him even a shred of attention. But the pair had been wholly occupied with Chris and Brenda. They hadn't appeared *that* critical during the ride back to the community.

Sure, Chris kept passing out, and that unhealthy shade of green he'd turned when Randy swerved to avoid the gates at the entrance to Lakeview, was off-putting. But he seemed fine now, all stitched up and chatting with Stone. Brenda had whimpered quietly for the entire trek. Abe had taken it as a sign of relief at being saved. Apparently, he was wrong.

And, he determined, if God truly loved him, He'd stifle Brenda's intermittent whaling.

At first, he held some empathy for her. The noise Brenda's clothing made as Lydia pealed it from her skin reminded Abe of a wet towel pulling from a sticky surface. Now, she was making him queasy as she shrieked with each piece of debris Jerry and Lydia removed from her wounds or when they dabbed them with antibiotic salve.

*Salve! I hate that word.*

As he sat shirtless, awaiting their attention, the bruising had spread unchecked; the icepack had only proven effective at soaking his sheets. He was wet, in pain, and cranky!

He shut his eyes, pulled as deep a breath as his angry ribs would allow, and leaned his head back. His pillow had grown warm and misshapen. "That's IT! I need a little help — OVER HERE!"

"Relax, Abe. Jerry'll be here in a second. They're finishing up with Brenda. But I've got some news."

"Stone," Abe's eyes opened slowly, "unless you have a syringe full of morphine, I suggest you stop speaking. Your voice hurts my side."

Stone muted his amusement with Abe's dramatics. "I'm sure you'll get something for the pain. Now, like I was saying, I talked to Chris. He told me about the attack... it was brutal. They lost eight people. But you need to hear something. He confirmed what you saw. Some *thing* was controlling the infected. He started to describe it, but passed out before he could finish. All he managed to say was that the thing was tall and half naked, just like you said."

Abe closed his eyes again. "Not good, Stone, not at all. If one of these ugly sticks has somehow evolved like the ones the military's looking for, we don't stand a chance."

"And who do we have here?"

Stone stepped away as Jerry arrived at Abe's bedside. "Nice of you to carve out some time for me, doc. I've probably already bled out... internally. But, hey, no worries as long as you've tidied up the young lady's scratch."

"I'll get Lu," Stone answered Jerry's pleading stare. "She'll keep him calm."

"I don't need calm. I need pain meds and a diagnosis. Anyway, she doesn't care. We drove right past her and she didn't even wave. And I'm sure Nic's told her about me by now. And do you see her? NO, you don't. Know why? She doesn't care — that's why!" Stone was already gone, but yelling felt good!

Abe's body jerked, his hands shot skyward, and his face twisted. "What in the actual hell is wrong with you?"

Jerry peered over the rim of his glasses. "I'm working on your diagnosis. That's what you asked me to do, right? Or did you just want to complain?"

Abe's head tilted in time with the fading pain. "You look familiar. Where do I know you from?" It was the way Jerry looked at him that triggered a fuzzy memory.

Jerry pressed hard on the bruise's crown, then shook his head as Abe howled. "So sorry, but I need to make certain my diagnosis is accurate."

Abe's complexion faded to fish belly, his breaths came in shallow gasps, and sweat beaded along his entire frame. "Whatever I did, I'm sorry."

Jerry feigned confusion and leaned in close. "By no means am I intentionally causing you pain, Abe. And, as for your apology, it's unnecessary. As you stated on that warm summer day last year, you were simply trying to protect the aesthetics of our neighborhood." Jerry pinched and twisted Abe's darkening skin. "And, I agree, hippies like me should be more thoughtful and, how did you phrase it? Oh, yes, mow our lawns more than once a year."

He jabbed Abe's ribs again and grinned at the man's mournful whale. "But, I'll tell you this, that fine you arranged with the city, well, that certainly helped my motivation. So much so that after my twenty-four-hour shifts responding to car accidents and heart attacks, I'd storm right out and clip that green stuff right up. I'd walk up and down my lawn smiling because I knew the neighborhood looked better and you were happy."

Abe's eyes rolled up, he searched for oxygen, couldn't focus on anything but searing pain. "I'm sorry," he croaked.

"Water under the proverbial bridge, my friend. Now, you save your energy, you'll need it to heal your broken rib. We'll wrap your chest and send you on your way."

"Pain. I need something for pain."

"Oh dear, did I forget to give you that shot? Must be the aftereffects of all that sun beating on my hippy head... while I was mowing my lawn."

\*\*\*

"He's a horrible person, Lu. I'm telling you, he tortured me. He's mad about something I don't even remember doing. He didn't give me any pain meds until after he tried to kill me!"

Abe's glassy-eyed stare and loopy tone made his accusations easy to dismiss, which she did while stuffing another pillow behind him, propping him as straight as possible. "Sure he was. Nasty 'ole hippy. Now, get some rest."

Abe's eyes went unfocused, his face slacked, and he pointed at Lu. "Even though you don't care, I still think you're a nice lady."

Lu rubbed his cropped hair and smiled as he snored softly. "And you're crazy."

# Chapter 44

Tommy's knuckles skipped across the alternator and slammed into the fan blade shroud. "Son of a bitch!"

"Snap the bolt?" Steve moved the flashlight beam to his face.

"Clean. Alright, we're out of time. We'll have to leave it. Kelly, Mark, grab what you can and toss it in the U-Haul. We'll ride with Steve and Kim."

He watched his wife and son pull their go-bags from the old Jeep Wrangler's open hatch, then shifted his gaze to the caravan stretching out behind them. How he became the leader of over sixty refugees was still a mystery, one he'd never unravel if he didn't get this ragtag group moving. "Should've stuck with my emergency plan and bugged to the cabin after the news showed infected streaming from Hopkins," he grumbled as he tossed the wrench into the toolbox.

His hunting cabin, in Central Ohio, was a solid two-hour ride on a good day. It had now been twenty-four hours and none of it had been good. *Should've taken main roads*!

They'd fortified a cluster of homes in a cul-de-sac a quarter mile outside the Lakeview subdivision's gates. The small numbers of infected they'd encountered early on were easily dealt with. But the numbers they witnessed yesterday equated to a force equal to an army battalion and drove home his deepest fear; these things were clustering into larger, more deadly groups. They bugged out the instant the monsters gave chase to whatever prey they'd caught wind of and had faced one setback after another. His 1987 Jeep Wrangler, his pride and joy, had just joined the list.

"We going to make it?"

"We'll make it, Steve. *When* is the question. If we don't hit any more roadblocks and avoid additional breakdowns, we'll be setting up camp by sunup."

Three muzzle flashes punctured the night air as Tommy stopped talking. Refugees at the far end of the caravan scrambled into defensive positions. They were spread thin and exposed — the infected had just exploited those weaknesses under cover of darkness.

"Kim, get out of here — go, now!" Tommy ran toward the fighting, ordering each vehicle along the way to follow Kim.

As he neared the battle, the challenge crystallized; dozens of infected had engulfed half the caravan. He shouldered his rifle, but living and infected flashed through his sights, freezing his finger as it tensed on the trigger. The pavement stretching the length of the caravan's rear contingent was littered with broken and twisted bodies. They'd been overrun before he even realized they were under attack.

Steve slid to a stop next to him and raised his rifle. "I don't have a clean shot!"

Tommy reached to his side and lowered the barrel of Steve's rifle. "We need to catch up to Kim and the others."

Steve's head snapped to face Tommy. "We can't just leave them to be slaughtered!"

Tommy inched forward. "They're already dead. Let's go!"

He rushed in the direction his family had traveled, shutting out the chaos behind. But taillights blazed not a hundred yards from where they'd been when he'd ordered the caravan's forward contingent to evacuate — they shouldn't be there. With each step, his gate quickened. Vehicle doors sat ajar. Shadows bounced through the red hue cast by the lights. His body exploded forward. His wife was screaming.

\*\*\*

Hidden in a small cluster of trees, his soldiers feasted on the bodies of the heavily damaged as he guarded the more viable of his new recruits. With their defenses weakened by fear and confusion and thinned by distance, this food had been easy to hunt. His army's ranks had swelled to numbers approaching what he would need to reach the food. Sampson's eyes closed; the fear within that building would taste like syrup.

## Chapter 45

Lu cringed as her house came into view. Nic was on the porch again, and her dour expression nearly spun Lu on her heel. *I'd rather sleep on the street!*

"How much longer?" Nic asked as Lu walked up the driveway.

"Three weeks."

A week had passed, and Lu was sure Nic was plotting to kill Abe in his sleep. Actually, she still questioned if Nic had tried to end him three days ago when he stumbled down the stairs with Nic behind him, offering to *help* him on his daily walk. It *was* possible.

"I'm going to live with Aislin. At least until Finn gets back."

"Can I come with you?" Lu was only half-kidding. "What's he like today?"

"Ornery, but I'm guessing it's not all about his *condition*. Can I tell you how much I hate when he says that? If we had a dentist, I'd knock his teeth straight out of his head."

"Finn?"

Nic nodded. "They deploy today. You'd think Abe's best friend moved to a different state the way he's acting. My guess is he's twisted because Finn hasn't reached out."

Lu gave a sad smile. She knew what Abe was going through. Nic was her best friend — had kept her sane since the beginning and now she was moving out.

"How was guard duty?" Nic asked, changing the subject.

"Meh, not much going on. Towers haven't reported a sighting in a couple days. It's like the infected have moved on. I've noticed we're dealing with our own community more. We need to work on a set of rules because the shit people are trying to get away with is unacceptable."

"Human nature. Cram a bunch of people together in a high stress environment, take away their creature comforts, and voila, instant asshole!"

Lu looked at her friend pleadingly. "Can you stay for dinner... please? I'll take him for his walk and lock him in our room. It'll be just you and me. I have a bottle of wine stashed, it'll be like old times."

Nic winked. "But I'm going to take a walk of my own. This is, hands down, the worst part of the day."

\*\*\*

"I'm telling you, Randy, they're hard to control and we'll burn through ammo too fast."

Lu tiptoed through the living room as Abe, from their bedroom, yelled at Randy about which guns they should use. It was a daily conversation — one of many. He'd radio each member of his team and berate them on a myriad of topics, but their choice of guns was his favorite.

"Those gorilla hands of yours... hey, Randy. You there? Randy? Answer me. I can't believe he turned his radio off! I hope he shoots himself."

Lu smirked. It ended the same way every time.

"Who's down there?"

Lu winced, she just wanted five minutes to herself before fighting with him about his walk.

"Nic, is that you? Answer me! I have a gun up here. Don't give me a reason to use it!"

"It's me, Abe. I didn't want to disturb your strategy session with Randy." She pulled a deep breath. "It's time for your walk."

"Already took one. We're good. Can you bring me a few more DVDs? Look for the *Resident Evil* movies. I'm doing some research."

"After your walk."

"I said I. Already. Took. A. Walk!"

"Abel Andrew Willings. When I get to the top of the stairs, your ass better be ready to go or I swear, as God as my witness, I'll punch you in your ribs! Have I made myself clear?"

"Damn, no reason to get nasty. I said I was ready to go. What's taking you so long?"

\*\*\*

Lu held the front door open, waiting for Abe to shuffle through. He was making progress, but still grumbled obscenities during the entirety of his walks.

She smirked when she got a clear look at his belly. He'd definitely put on a few pounds. She held her commentary. Instead, saving it for a kill shot during an argument.

"Do you hear that?"

*Ears like a rabbit.* "What, moaning and groaning? Can't get away from it, Abe."

"Shush. Sounds like a copter.... it is!" Abe's shuffle accelerated while he craned his neck skyward. "Sounds like more than one."

Lu couldn't help herself, and grinned as her husband trundled to the middle of their yard and watched the sky like a little boy.

"They're coming, Lu," he shouted as he waved for her to join him. "Black Hawks, four of them!"

His eyes widened as the formation entered the community's airspace. Three of them peeled off and lingered above the barrier's southeast corner while one slowed to a hover directly above him.

Abe shielded his eyes as the bird's down draft flattened the unkempt lawn around him. *Was that a dog barking?* He strained to hear, but the thumping rotor blades drowned the world in swirling wind and power.

A blue plastic bag shot from the Hawk's open troop hold and rocketed to earth. Abe tried to move, to dodge from the bag's path, but he was too slow. The bag thumped to the ground by his toes and shot into his calf.

His scream, mercifully overpowered by the Hawk's turbine, stretched until Lu handed him the bag. "It's for you," she yelled as the copter gained altitude, lessening its downdraft and cutting back slightly on its roar.

Abe's brow furrowed as he took the bag from Lu and reached in. It remained crinkled as he read the message scribbled on the baseball's dimpled leather.

*I'll bring you some bacon.* Then, in the baseball's sweet spot. *You're a good man!*

Abe looked skyward and searched the opening for his friend, but the Black Hawk was already sliding away. His chest puffed painfully as he straightened his spine and saluted.

## Chapter 46

Li dangled from the pilothouse's rigging, watching his force swarm over the ship's deck. If he could keep them from ripping one another apart, they would be unstoppable.

But their rage radiated from the deck, the blinding, all-consuming rage coursing through them. Life had taken an uncomplicated path; cull the weak to protect the species.

As their armada entered the Luzon Strait, with the Philippine Sea only miles away, Li hoisted his simmering body to the *Yan'an's* pilothouse observation gangway and peered through its thick glass. Capitan Yun glared back. The man's neck was a roadmap of pulsing veins, his teeth clenched, and his knuckles white from pressure. Li snarled. The captain looked like his other soldiers — a razor's edge from destroying those around him.

Li spun to face the sea. He leaned his drenched body into the salty air and closed his eyes. It had taken only a month to crush his country's pathetic leaders.

Soon, the world would tremble at his feet. And they would taste his boot.

Next From Bryan Dean:

Zero: Abel's Apocalypse Book Three

Also From Bryan Dean:

Zombie Fungus: Abel's Apocalypse Book One

Reviews are invaluable to independent writers. Please consider leaving yours where you purchased this book.

Feel free to like me on Facebook at Abel's Apocalypse. You'll be the first notified of specials and new releases.

## ABOUT THE AUTHOR

Hailing from Cleveland, Ohio, Bryan still lives in NEO (Northeast Ohio). A fan of all things creepy, except birds, Alfred Hitchcock ruined birds for him. He sees a horror story in every moment of every day. But simply doesn't have time to write them all down. He learned how to tell stories by talking himself out of trouble as a young man.

After spending years in corporate America, where he developed his crusty exterior, he decided it was time to do something he's always wanted to do. You're reading it or should be, so stop reading this and buy his book.

Made in the USA
Monee, IL
09 November 2023